"Where does that leave us?" he asked

"Seven years younger."

"And seven years hungrier." His legs closed around her, holding her in place, and his hands sought her curls, threading his fingers through them as he brought her mouth to his. His taste and touch and smell were all familiar, blending with memory, more than memory, much much more.

"In seven years, there was nothing I wanted as much as this," Shane whispered, his mouth at her ear.

"I'd wake up at night someitmes, dreaming that you were kissing me." Wendy leaned against him, her hands on his shoulders. "And I'd hate myself for dreaming."

"It's not too late." Shane's arms tightened around her. "You still melt against me, fairy child."

"But that's not enough, is it?"

Dear Reader,

Although our culture is always changing, the desire to love and be loved is a constant in every woman's heart. Silhouette Romances reflect that desire, sweeping you away with books that will make you laugh and cry, poignant stories that will move you time and time again.

This year we're featuring Romances with a playful twist. Remember those fun-loving heroines who always manage to get themselves into tricky predicaments? You'll enjoy reading about their escapades in Silhouette Romances by Brittany Young, Debbie Macomber, Annette Broadrick and Rita Rainville.

We're also publishing Romances by many of your all-time favorites such as Ginna Gray, Diana Palmer and Joan Hohl. Your overwhelming reaction to these authors has served as a touchstone for us, and we're pleased to bring you more books with Silhouette's distinctive medley of charm, wit and—above all—*romance*. I hope you enjoy this book, and the many stories to come.

Sincerely,

Rosalind Noonan
Senior Editor
SILHOUETTE BOOKS

EMILIE RICHARDS
Sweet Mockingbird's Call

Silhouette Romance

Published by Silhouette Books New York

America's Publisher of Contemporary Romance

SILHOUETTE BOOKS
300 E. 42nd St., New York, N.Y. 10017

ISBN: 0-373-08441-2

First Silhouette Books printing June 1986

America's Publisher of Contemporary Romance

Printed in the U.S.A.

Books by Emilie Richards

Silhouette Romance

Brendan's Song #372
Sweet Georgia Gal #393
Gilding the Lily #401
Sweet Sea Spirit #413
Angel and the Saint #429
Sweet Mockingbird's Call #441

EMILIE RICHARDS

grew up in St. Petersburg and attended college in northern Florida. She also fell in love there and married her husband, Michael, who is her opposite in every way. "The only thing that we agreed on was that we were very much in love. We haven't changed our minds about that in the sixteen years we've been together." They now live in New Orleans with four children, who span from toddler to teenager.

The MacDonald Family - Hall County, Georgia

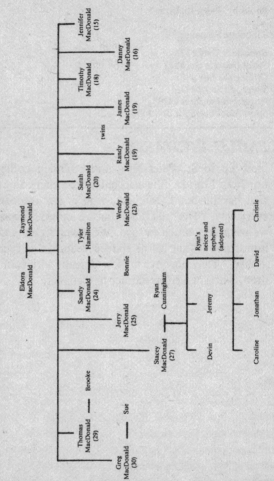

Chapter One

The pastel roses lying in neatly arranged piles on the porch of the Georgia farmhouse were as incongruous as a diamond tiara on a scarecrow. The farmhouse was overgrown, sprawling in every direction as if the carpenters who had added on to it had chosen at random the places where new rooms were to be built. Freshly painted and in good repair, the house still resembled a friendly barn. The fragile roses were a sharp contrast. The young woman arranging them in a green glass vase was a contrast, too.

Wendy MacDonald's slender body was curved comfortably against the carved porch banister, and her long fingers wove in and out of the flowers, adjusting and readjusting them as if she performed a ritual of supreme importance. Her simple pink sundress billowed slightly in the cool breeze, and she tucked it smoothly beneath her in an absentminded feminine gesture. She was both out of place and completely comfortable in the simple setting. Out of place because she looked as if she would be suited to more formal surroundings; comfortable because the sprawling farmhouse was the only home she had ever known.

Twenty-three years under the Georgia sun and a life filled with farm chores and the arguments and laughter of eleven brothers and sisters had not diminished Wendy's natural poise. Sandy MacDonald Hamilton, one of Wendy's two older sisters, liked to say that Wendy was a beautiful butterfly in a family of honeybees. Sarah MacDonald, one of Wendy's two younger sisters, liked to say that their mother had been in such a hurry to get home from the hospital after Wendy's birth that she had grabbed the wrong baby by mistake.

For a moment Wendy's hands stilled as she lifted her head to aim a question at the front screen door. "What do you think? Should I get another vase or should I just fill this one until it explodes?"

"Fill the vase full," Sarah said, pushing the wheezing screen door as she came out on the porch from the living room where she had been observing her sister. "That way you won't have to get up and find another one."

Wendy's mouth lifted lazily at the corners. She was used to Sarah's utter practicality. Twenty-year-old Sarah never wasted a moment, a syllable or an emotion. She was a walking encyclopedia of facts, as down-to-earth and sensible as a computer. The two sisters were opposites in every way. "I should have known that's what you'd say," Wendy teased. She sorted through the roses, choosing three of the prettiest, and held them out to her sister. "Here, put these in a vase in your room. You need something to remind you that the world's full of more than statistics."

Sarah took the roses with a crooked smile. She was practical but not humorless. No one raised in the noisy, rambunctious MacDonald household could have survived without a sense of humor. She flopped down on a rocking chair, still holding the roses, and watched Wendy continue her arrangement.

The sun was sending a steady golden glow to the front steps where Wendy sat, setting fire to the white-gold of her short curls. The sun enhanced rather than detracted from the dusty rose of Wendy's complexion and the intense brown of her eyes, but it also highlighted the tiny mouth with the full bottom lip that kept her from being considered classically beautiful. It was Wendy's own judgment that she should have been born when Clara Bow was the model against which all women measured themselves.

"No matter what you're doing, you always look as if you're in training to become the First Lady," Sarah said with a shake of her head. "Darned if I can figure out how you manage it."

"I'm not in training to become anybody's lady."

"You realize that's a terrible waste, don't you? Somewhere there's an upwardly mobile executive who needs you to grace his home. You could live a life of luxury, have 2.3 children and a matched set of Irish wolfhounds."

"But I'd have to have a husband, too. And that part doesn't appeal to me at all. Ouch!" Wendy sucked on her finger where a thorn from one of the roses had punctured it. "See what talking about marriage does to me?"

"You're a mystery to me. And I love mysteries."

The screen door wheezed again, and Mrs. MacDonald came out on the porch to join her two daughters. Perching on the opposite side of the steps from Wendy, she lifted the hair off the back of her neck to let the spring breeze caress her damp skin. "Smell those magnolia blossoms."

Wendy reached across the space separating her from her mother and patted Eldora MacDonald's knee. "When I move to Atlanta, that's one of the things I'll miss the most."

"They have magnolias in Atlanta," Sarah pointed out.

"I know. What I'll miss is hearing Ma say 'smell those magnolia blossoms.'" Wendy smiled at her mother. "You've always been the one who reminds us to stop and enjoy what we have."

"And you've always been the one who takes the time to do it." Mrs. MacDonald smiled back at her daughter. "Thank goodness you're not leaving for the city right away. You kids are all growing up so fast the house is going to be empty in no time."

"Six kids at home is hardly empty," Sarah said, leaning her head against the back of the rocker and closing her eyes. "But I'm glad Wendy isn't leaving yet. There'll be more help with the dishes."

Wendy laughed and the sound was competition for the birds in the big magnolia tree that towered over the front porch. "Are you trying to tell me I can be easily replaced by a dishwasher?"

"Not easily. Ma refuses to have one. I've been trying to convince her for years that the cost of the hot water and soap we use more than makes up for the—"

"Enough!" Mrs. MacDonald held up her hands in mock protest.

"Well, I'm not glad that I have to put off my plans for another season, but I am glad I can help Mrs. Merritt with the shop," Wendy said, placing another rose in her arrangement. "I'm just so sorry that she's having trouble with her heart again. I hope a summer doing nothing will help her get her strength back."

"She works too hard in that gift shop," said Mrs. MacDonald, who always worked too hard herself. "She's too old for all that aggravation. It's a good thing she had the sense to hire you when you were still a college student. Now you know the business."

"Yes. I was the obvious choice to take over Melange for the summer." Wendy pushed the last rose in place.

"You may be the obvious choice, but you still didn't have to do it. I'm proud of you for making the sacrifice."

"Well, Atlanta will still be waiting for me unless the Yankees burn it to the ground again." Wendy held the flower arrangement out to her mother. "What do you think?"

"I think the chance that the Yankees will burn it down again are slight." Mrs. MacDonald laughed at Wendy's grimace. "The roses are beautiful, honey. You've always had such a way with arranging things."

"Wendy could make an outhouse look like something out of *Better Homes and Gardens*," Sarah said matter-of-factly to her mother. "Whatever artistic skill was available in your genes all went to her, along with the curly hair."

"And who got the photographic memory and gold eyes big enough to make a prospector greedy?" Wendy complimented her sister. She watched Sarah's myriad freckles dance as their owner grinned.

"Well, the photographic memory isn't getting much of a workout this summer, though the big gold eyes are. Sitting in the shade of a clump of scrubby pine trees and counting the cars that go by for the Georgia Department of Transportation isn't exactly an intellectual pursuit."

"I'll bet you're finding some way of keeping yourself busy." Wendy hadn't lived with Sarah for Sarah's twenty years without understanding a little of the way her sister's mind worked. Sarah could take a job that would have turned Wendy into a mindless idiot and finish with enough information to write a dissertation.

"Actually it's interesting if you like to spy on people. I bet I know more about what happens in this part of the county than anyone else does. I'm privy to all kinds of interesting insights."

"Sandy always said you had a potential career as an F.B.I. agent," Mrs. MacDonald said, enjoying the byplay between her two daughters. She missed her two oldest girls, Stacey and Sandy, who were both married and living in other parts of the South. She wanted to take advantage of the remaining time with these two daughters who also would be gone soon.

"What interesting information did you learn today?" Wendy asked Sarah as she brushed away a lacy-winged dragonfly who was trying valiantly to make a home on the roses.

"Well, Mr. Brandt from down the road is driving a brand-new fire-engine-red pickup these days." Sarah waved her hand in front of her face lazily. "The Kents have relatives staying with them, and the Woodrows left for Florida yesterday."

"Now how would you know where they went?"

"They had Florida or Bust scribbled in the dust on the back of their station wagon." Sarah waited for the chuckles to die down. "I learned something even more interesting, though. I found out that you can take the man off the farm, but you can't take the farm from the man."

"A riddle." Wendy pretended to think about Sarah's words. "I'll need a hint before I can decipher that one."

"Are you talking about Shane Reynolds?" Mrs. MacDonald turned to Sarah, and she missed the sight of the color leaving Wendy's cheeks at her words.

"Precisely. But how did you know?"

"I've been waiting for him to come back now that his father is dead. He's always loved that land like it was part of him."

"Well, he's here," Sarah said. "I saw him drive by three times yesterday. I meant to tell you at dinner last night, but I forgot."

"How did you know it was him?" Mrs. MacDonald asked. "You were just a young teenager when he left. It was a long time ago. Must be five, six years."

"Seven." Wendy's voice when she interrupted was hollow although she was attempting to sound normal. "It was seven years ago." She didn't add that it was almost seven years to the day. She had revealed enough.

"I never forget a face," Sarah said blithely. "And that's one face no female, even a thirteen-year-old female, could forget. He's still the same gorgeous man, only he's more a man than he was then."

"I'm sure you remember Shane," Mrs. MacDonald said, turning back to look at Wendy.

"Quite well."

"Seems to me he used to single you out for attention when he'd come over to see the boys. He used to call you— let's see if I can remember—he used to call you . . ."

"Fairy child." Wendy didn't quite meet her mother's eyes although Eldora MacDonald was too lost in thought to notice. "Shane Reynolds had quite a way with words." Stretching her legs to the steps below her, she stood. "I've just realized what's missing in this arrangement. It needs some ferns to balance it out. I think I'll go see what I can find in the woods."

"Looks perfect to me," Sarah said.

Wendy tried to smile but found she was unable. "It will look even better when I'm done." She turned and started down the steps.

"Wendy?" Her daughter's ruffled calm had finally penetrated Mrs. MacDonald's reverie. "Are you all right, honey?"

"Fine, Ma. I'll be back in a little while." Without turning, Wendy started down the path through the yard to the fifteen-acre stand of trees bordering their property.

The woods, which had been ablaze with flowering dogwood just a month before, were now a sedate haven of different shades of green. Wendy let her feet carry her to the spot where she knew she would have her choice of ferns. Mechanically she picked a handful and stared unseeingly at them until she realized just how ridiculous her stance was. She set the ferns on a rock to collect later and continued to wander through the woods, toward the edge of the MacDonald farm.

Shane Reynolds was back. She shouldn't have been surprised. Shane was back, and she was leaving.

Actually his timing was only off by a few months. Had he waited until September, she never would have needed to worry about facing him again. In September she would be settled in Atlanta, enjoying the luxuries and benefits of city life. Surely then her memories of Shane Reynolds would diminish until, even if she saw him again, they wouldn't matter. Surely then the mere mention of his name would no longer cause a painful internal avalanche of sensations.

Shane Reynolds. He was no longer the twenty-year-old boy-man whom she remembered so vividly. He was twenty-seven now, fully grown, although according to Sarah he was no less attractive for it. But then she was no longer the sixteen-year-old fairy child who had captivated his attention that night so many years before. She hadn't been a child for years. Shane had seen to that.

"Do you even remember, Shane?" she asked out loud. Her voice was a fierce whisper taken immediately by the wind and dispersed among the spring-budding trees.

Her answer was the sound of a horse's hooves on the red clay road running along the edge of the farm. It was a distant sound, evoking memories that wouldn't be denied. Wendy sank to a log lying on the ground at her feet and, against her will, she remembered.

She had been thirteen when she began to fall in love with Shane Reynolds. It had been a day much like this one, but hotter, the summer sun biting through the shade of the oaks and poplars to remind her that she should be home helping her mother begin supper preparations. She had escaped the noise and confusion of her family to come to the woods and dream, and now it was time to face them again, fortified.

Her hair had hung in ringlets past her shoulders, and her body, just beginning to develop, had been clad in cutoff shorts and a ruffled halter top. The sound of a horse's hooves had interrupted her return, and she had pushed through the thick stand of trees by the road to see who was coming.

"Shane!" She had waved excitedly at the boy riding a chestnut quarter horse without benefit of saddle or bridle. "Shane!"

"Hi, Wendy." The boy stopped his horse on the road in front of her and waited until she could catch up. Wendy was just at the age where boys and horses were tied in her heart for first place. But in any such competition, Shane Reynolds won hands down. At seventeen, he had outgrown any teenage gangliness and already showed signs of becoming an appealing man. His fine brown hair and blue eyes were a sharp contrast to his bronzed skin and high cheekbones. Not particularly tall, he carried himself with innate pride and masculine grace. It was a combination few females could resist. Even Wendy had heard stories of his exploits with the girls of the local high school.

Somehow it hadn't mattered. She had grown up with Shane. He had played and fought with her brothers, eaten numerous meals at the family table, teased all her sisters and generally been a pain in the neck. She didn't quite understand the way her heart beat a little faster now when she was near him, or the reasons why she found excuses to talk to him when she could. She only knew that Shane was special, and on that hot, summer day, that had been enough of a reason to stop him.

"Can I ride home with you?"

Shane had looked at her for a long moment, assessing the way her long legs looked under the skimpy cutoffs and the way her slender body was beginning to blossom. "It's unusual to see you without an army of brothers surrounding you," he said.

"When you have as many brothers as I do, all the togetherness is understandable," she reasoned, wondering why Shane was smiling at her words.

"Now do you really think that's why they stick so close to you?" Shane guided his horse to the side of the road by a boulder. "Come on up."

Wendy scampered to the top of the boulder and took the tanned hand that was held out to her. In a minute she was sitting in front of Shane and they were moving slowly down the road.

She had ridden bareback with friends and with her siblings. It was not a new experience. But sitting in front of Shane, his arms casually surrounding her, his hard, young body rubbing against hers, she had been swallowed by a host of new sensations. And she hadn't been experienced enough to worry about them. "This feels wonderful!"

"Do you really think your brothers stay so close by accident, Wendy?"

She had felt Shane's arms tighten a little, and she had leaned back to rest against him. "Sure. What do you think?"

"I think they know what a little treasure you are."

She hadn't understood. "No. They think I'm a little nuisance."

He had laughed, then, and she had laughed too, glad that she had made him happy.

"You're a fairy child," Shane said. "A sprite, a magic little wood nymph."

"If I were, I'd make you take me riding every day. I'd capture you and make you do whatever I wanted."

"I think you might be able to do that anyway."

Wendy had been pleased by the husky note in his voice, and she had snuggled against him a little more. The rest of their ride was silent until they reached the turnoff to the MacDonald farmhouse.

"Down you go," Shane said.

"But why?"

"Because I don't want your brothers angry with me."

His answer had surprised her, and she had swung one leg over the side of the horse to sit so that she could see Shane's face. "But my brothers like you."

"They won't like me for long if they think I'm interested in their little sister."

Her heart had beat faster than she had known it could. "Are you interested in me?" There had been nothing provocative about her question. She had just wanted to know.

"You'll find, fairy child, that there will hardly be a man in the county who isn't interested in you. But you're too young to understand that, aren't you?"

She had been puzzled. "But I asked if you were interested?"

"I think I'll answer that question in about five or six years." Shane had touched the tip of her nose with his fingertip. "But don't grow up too fast." Then he had bent his head and gently covered her mouth with his. And forever after, the sound of horses' hooves would be mixed with the sweet elation she had felt at her first real kiss.

Now Wendy sat close to the spot where she had seen Shane so many years before, holding her breath as she waited for the distant horse and rider to materialize. It had been a dry spring, and the lazy beat of hooves stirred a red cloud of dust, obscuring a clear view until they were a hundred yards away.

It was Shane. But then, somehow, she had known it would be. She was so immersed in memories that it could not have been anyone else. It was almost as if she had called him forth, out of her memory, to reexamine him.

He had the same proud posture, but his shoulders were wider. His chest was bare, his blue chambray shirt was unbuttoned to reveal dark, taut skin covering well honed muscles. His light brown hair, fine and straight, was shorter than she remembered it, but it skimmed his forehead. She remembered all too well how it felt to run her fingers through it, pushing it back to reveal the broad, jutting lines of his brow.

Shane melted into his sleek gray mount as if he were one with the powerful animal. Both horse and rider exuded a primitive tension as if neither were satisfied with the slow pace that was their mutual trial. Both seemed tensed to spring at the first provocation.

Why did people insist that memory covered up flaws? Wendy had sometimes wondered when she confronted Shane Reynolds again if she would discover that he was not the model of perfection that she remembered. Now she had her answer. He was better than her memories. His rugged bone structure and copper-tinged skin were a heritage from his mother who had been half-Cherokee, his blue eyes and light hair a gift from his father who had never given him anything else willingly. He had been an impressive boy. As a man he was superb.

Wendy was hidden by the trees, but Shane stopped directly in front of her as if he knew that he was being watched. She remembered that he had always had a sixth sense, an intuitive ability that gave him insight that other people lacked. Perhaps it was that insight now, or perhaps it was the surfacing of a long-forgotten memory that caused him to turn his horse toward the woods where she sat, breath held, as she waited for him to move on.

She forced herself to remain calm. He could not know that he was being watched. She tried to examine him coolly, to dissect his features and reveal some hidden flaw. But his flaws were too well hidden to see. She knew them well. His major one, consummate selfishness, had almost ruined her life.

There was a part of her that wanted to step out from under the cover of the trees and face him. There was another part that never wanted to face him again. She sat without moving and waited for him to leave. When he finally turned his horse loose to gallop down the road, she took a deep breath to chase his image from her mind.

Shane Reynolds was back. Perhaps it was inevitable that he would surface again. But she was not the same person. She had been sixteen when last she had encountered him. Now she was seven years older and a hundred years wiser. Standing, she brushed crumbled bark off the skirt of her dress and turned to go back to the house.

At the boulder where she had left the ferns, she bent to gather them. They had curled into tight knots, and they were turning brown before her eyes.

"And so it was with my life when you left me, Shane," she said as she scattered the ferns in the light breeze. "But never again. Never, never again."

Chapter Two

Wendy was flipping the ends of her curls with a round hard-bristled brush the next morning when Sarah knocked and entered her bedroom.

"Aren't you going to church? Everyone's just about ready."

"I just have to slip on a dress." Wendy pulled off her long quilted robe and dropped it on the bed before she walked to the closet. In a moment a buttercup jersey hugged her slender body, and she turned to Sarah for help with her zipper.

"You're never this late." Sarah's comment accompanied the rasping sound of the zipper.

Whether she should attend church at all that day had been a difficult decision. Wendy had slept normally, refusing to let Shane Reynolds interfere with her rest. She had allowed herself one haunting reminiscence in the woods, but then she had put her memories back in storage. It had been a shock to find that Shane was back, but it was one she could cope with. At least that's what she had told herself until it came time to get ready for church, and she realized that Shane might attend, too.

As a child and teenager, Shane had always come to church alone. Harnett Reynolds had insisted that his son go every Sunday although Harnett had never graced the tiny white building with his own presence. Shane had usually come in late to slide into one of the pews where the MacDonald family was sitting. Wendy clearly remembered some of the profane pranks that Shane and Thomas, one of her older brothers, had indulged in during services.

The building held memories of Shane that were as much a part of its interior as the shining brown pews or the simple rose-colored windows. It was the very same church that her sixteen-year-old imagination had decorated with flowers for a wedding that was never to take place.

"I just had trouble waking myself up this morning, but I'm ready now," she told Sarah, moving to the mirror to fasten a tiny gold hoop in each ear.

Sarah observed her sister with a curious eye. "You've been very quiet since yesterday afternoon."

"I've just been thinking about how much I want to move to Atlanta, I guess." Wendy took a deep breath and turned to face Sarah. "We'd better go."

The church was full of the familiar faces with whom Wendy had grown up. It never ceased to amaze her that in a world so full of trouble and turmoil, the same dear people would come together Sunday after Sunday to hear messages of hope and goodwill. It was another of the many things she would miss when she left home.

Although they had come in separate cars, the family sat together as they always had. On holidays, when everyone was home with their spouses and children, the Mac-

Donalds took up pew after pew. But today, with only part of the family present, they squeezed into a row at the back of the church with Wendy on the end.

Wendy shut her eyes and tried to absorb the peace and serenity of her surroundings. Shane was not there. She had worried needlessly. Harnett Reynolds was no longer alive to force his unwilling son to sit through a service that meant nothing to him. She would have days, perhaps weeks, before she was forced to face him. By then the shock of his reappearance would have worn off, and her defenses would be firmly in place.

But now, with the soft hum of familiar voices and the drone of electric fans stirring the air, her defenses were wobbly at best. Once again, it was too easy to envision the past. With a will of their own, her memories returned.

After Shane kissed her for the first time, Wendy had developed a full-scale crush on him. She saw him frequently, though never alone, and when she did, he was courtly and considerate, treating her with a mature respect that was completely different from the way her brothers treated her.

Sensing that she would become a family joke if anyone suspected her feelings for Shane, Wendy had forced herself to act naturally around him. No one noticed that she always managed to sit beside him when he was invited to stay for supper. And no one noticed that although Shane had nicknames for all the MacDonald girls, "fairy child" was said just a little differently.

Shane went away to the University of Georgia the year Wendy turned fifteen. Because his relationship with his father was strained at best, he didn't often appear for weekends. Wendy was in high school by then. She enjoyed the attention of the boys in her classes, and she enjoyed the increasing freedom and responsibility of growing up, but most of all, she enjoyed knowing that soon she would be old enough to begin dating Shane.

Wendy's parents were strict. At fifteen she wasn't allowed to date by herself. And as much as the MacDonalds liked Shane, Wendy would not have been allowed to date him under any circumstances. As a friend to their sons, Shane was perfectly acceptable. As a date for Wendy, he was out of the question.

No one thought that Shane was bad, but he had been raised in a home without love, and his response had been rebellion. Shane's reputation with the local girls was clouded and suspect. Wendy understood that until she was old enough to prove to her parents that Shane cared about her and wouldn't take advantage of her, she had no chance of being with him.

She waited patiently, enjoying her adolescence, putting Shane out of her mind when she could. She often wondered if he was waiting, too. It never occurred to her that he had been teasing on that bright summer day. Somehow she knew that Shane had meant his words. It only remained to be seen if he had changed his mind.

Then one day the summer before Wendy's junior year, she found out that Shane hadn't changed his mind at all.

He had come home to work for his father for the summer. The Reynolds' farm was only one of Harnett Reynolds's vast business interests. The love and energy Shane's father should have reserved for his motherless son had been put into real estate and local industry, in addition to the seven-hundred-acre farm where Shane had grown up. It was only this obsession with making money that kept Harnett busy enough so that it was tolerable for Shane to come back.

At first Wendy rarely saw him. Like all the MacDonald children she was busy helping her parents with the farm.

When Shane did visit, they were always surrounded by her brothers and sisters. But one day in August he found her alone.

She had been given the job of entertaining the youngest MacDonald children that afternoon, and they had spent hours jumping from the loft into piles of sweet-smelling hay in the barn. Finally tiring of their game, the children had wandered off to help their father feed chickens. Wendy had thrown open the huge windows in the loft to perch on the windowsill when she saw Shane's car approach. Her wave caught his eye. No one else was around, and in a minute he had climbed the ladder to join her.

It was almost as if three years had not passed. "My brothers aren't guarding me today," she said with a welcoming smile.

"I can see that."

"I'm growing up, too," she said.

"I can see that you are."

She continued to perch in the window, welcoming his inspection. She had cut her childish mop of unruly ringlets and the resulting curls were a halo around her maturing face. At that moment, with straw clinging to them, and her checked blouse tied in a knot at her midriff, she was a country angel.

"How many other boys have you kissed?" Shane asked finally, with a sigh.

"Just a few. For practice."

Shane held out his arms and she moved into them with an innocent trust that must have surprised him. This time, the kiss was different. Still gentle, it sparked feelings in her body that were totally alien. No amount of practice would have prepared her for the way she felt when Shane finally pushed her away.

"I hear your mother calling you," he said.

"Are you still waiting for me to grow up?"

"Not very patiently, I'm afraid. You don't suppose you could hurry a little, do you?" He smiled down at her and his hand lifted to brush the straw from her curls.

"I'll work on it." She stepped back, her face filled with regret. "I have to go."

"Yes, you do."

She almost skipped to the edge of the loft, her feet light, her body even lighter. When she was a few steps down the ladder, she lifted her head for one last glimpse of Shane's face. On an impulse she blew him a kiss. His grin was the last thing she saw before she ran out of the barn to find her mother....

"Wendy!"

Wendy surfaced slowly. She had been lost in her thoughts, and it was only when she felt the sharp dig of Sarah's elbow in her side that she opened her eyes and remembered where she was. "What?"

"Shane Reynolds is here," Sarah whispered.

Wendy kept her eyes straight ahead. Her body temperature felt as though it had dropped ten degrees. Her hands were icy and to her utter despair, trembling. Where was the hard-won sophistication that she had battled for years to attain? Who was this young woman who could be so overwhelmed by one mistake in her past that she dissolved when confronted with it?

As one body, Wendy's family turned to welcome the newcomer. Only Wendy kept her eyes straight ahead. By doing so she knew that sharp-eyed Sarah would comprehend why her sister had been so quiet for the past twenty-four hours.

"Move over, Wendy." The voice in her ear was deep and unmistakable. That Shane would have the arrogance to sit beside her stiffened Wendy's spine. Without turning her head she moved a few, barely discernible inches. Not moving farther was a mistake. She should have realized that her obvious reluctance would only tantalize him. He made a space for himself by branding her thigh with his and pushing her toward Sarah. She could not cause a scene by leaving the pew nor could she move away from him. She was caught between the man she least wanted to be near and the sister whose suspicions were probably developing at the speed of light.

Wendy could feel Shane's arm resting casually behind her on the wooden pew. The heat of his body so intimately against hers was achingly familiar. It was too much to bear just to cool Sarah's curiosity. Turning slightly she faced him. She was not surprised to find that he was looking at her.

"There are other places for you to sit, Shane Reynolds."

"Nowhere else quite this appealing."

Up close he was not the same. Maturity had give his face a new depth and sensual appeal that had only been hinted at when he was twenty. He was a man destined to improve with age.

His voice was different, too. Never before had it been sardonic when addressing her. Now it was. The expression in his eyes was also unfamiliar. The pale-blue irises were filled with cold dislike. It was a perfect match for the dislike in her brown ones.

"You always were good at doing just exactly what you wanted." She had managed to keep her voice casual. She shifted her body to pull it as far from his as possible and turned to face the front of the church again. In a minute the preacher was in the pulpit and everyone quieted. Wendy tried to look calm when Shane was asked to stand to be welcomed back into the congregation. Then they all stood to sing the first hymn of the morning.

It was inevitable that they would have to share a hymn book. The situation was absurd. They stood together, Shane's baritone blending with Wendy's soprano, as if nothing had ever passed between them. They stood together, shoulders and hips touching, as if they had never been anything except friends. Wendy had never felt so strongly that she was living a lie.

Sitting next to Shane for the entire service would have been unbearable, but she was spared the necessity. Ten minutes into the service she began to rise to leave with the children who were going to their Sunday school classes.

"Leaving already?" Shane's hand on her arm detained her. To anyone watching the gesture was casually friendly. Only Wendy would feel the steel bite of his fingers as they dug into her arm.

"I'm helping the kindergarten teacher." She was forced to look at him. His expression mocked her words. "Excuse me, please," she said pleasantly, trying unsuccessfully to pull her arm from his grasp.

"I want to talk to you after church." Shane's voice was low and for her ears only.

Wendy lowered her lashes and allowed herself a small smile. "You can't always get what you want, Shane," she said softly. "But you probably haven't had occasion to learn that, have you?"

"I'll see you after the service." His fingers slid carelessly down her arm before he let her go. Wendy stood and squeezed in front of him, her legs brushing his knees. She walked proudly from the church, smiling at the children who were racing ahead to their classes. Only she was aware of the sick feeling in the pit of her stomach that promised to stay with her for the rest of the day.

It was simple to find ways of staying busy after the service. Jennifer, Wendy's fifteen-year-old sister and the youngest MacDonald, came into the kindergarten class to announce that mice had been nesting in the supply closet.

Wendy graciously volunteered to clean and reorganize the closet after church. It was the perfect excuse to avoid Shane. She sent Jennifer to tell her parents not to expect her back until it was time for their traditional Sunday afternoon dinner. Then she attacked the closet with the fury of all her pent-up frustrations. When she was finally finished with it, enough time had elapsed to assure her that she would not encounter Shane. She knew that he would not have had the patience to wait for her. Shane's patience had always been in short supply.

She stopped by the preacher's study to tell him she was leaving, and then she stepped out into the parking lot. Some things never changed. And some things did. Shane was standing beside the battered pickup of a local farmer, his foot propped on the back bumper, his hand on the tailgate. Without hearing a word of the conversation, Wendy knew they were discussing crops or weather or poultry. It would have been a familiar, friendly scene if it had been anyone but Shane.

She walked to her car with her head stiffly forward. She didn't wave or smile, but it didn't matter. By the time she reached her car, Shane had reached it, too. He leaned casually against the door with his arms folded, watching her.

"So, Shane," she said without preamble. "You got what you wanted after all."

"What I wanted was simply to find out how you are."

Wendy took the time to examine him while she swallowed the heated words that were threatening to erupt at any moment. *You're seven years too late,* she wanted to scream at him. Instead she swept him with a frozen glance.

He had been too close this morning to inspect. Now she saw that he was wearing a beautifully tailored blue suit that set off his dark skin and pale eyes. His shirt was crisp and white, his tie the finest silk. He wore the clothes with the aplomb of someone used to expensive things. Finally her eyes found his face.

"I'm fine, thank you."

"Now common courtesy demands that you ask me the same question."

"So we're playing by new rules. Common courtesy was never included in the old ones." Her words made no impression on him, and she was angry at her own sarcasm. Everything she said rang with the hurt she thought she had put behind her. "How are you?" she forced herself to ask as politely as possible.

"Glad to be home."

Common courtesy demanded that she say, "We're glad to have you back," but the words wouldn't even begin to form. Wendy dug in her purse for her car keys. "I'd like to leave, if you don't mind."

"I thought you'd be married by now. I hear Stacey and Sandy are."

"They are." Wendy's eyes didn't waver as she met his. "I don't intend to marry."

"A pity."

Wendy sunk her teeth into her bottom lip as Shane's eyes leisurely found every visible part of her body. His examination was an insult. "Do you intend to stay here?" she asked, her voice one step from an audible sneer.

"Stay here? In Hall County? Yes. I do. Why? Do you want me to leave?"

"It doesn't matter to me. I'm leaving myself in September." She stepped slightly forward, but he didn't move.

"We'll have to get together to talk over old times before you go."

"No we won't."

"But we have some catching up to do." His voice was heavy with irony. "It's been seven years, almost to the day, since I saw you last."

The sophisticated game came to a abrupt halt. That he could stand there and casually mention the last time they had seen each other seemed diabolical. Wendy's carefully fortified defenses tumbled like the walls of Jericho. All she wanted from life, at that moment, was to hurt him.

"Do you mark your calendar, Shane? Do you circle the date in red and seduce someone every year on that date as a salute to our anniversary?" Her eyes filled with angry tears, and she turned her back on him to avoid giving even more of her feelings away. She clenched her arms to her chest as if to keep herself from exploding into a million tiny pieces.

"Wendy—"

"Damn you, Shane Reynolds." Her musical voice was harsh with emotion. "Get out of here. We have nothing to say to each other!"

"Maybe not right now. But soon." His words were a warning. They echoed in Wendy's head long after the sound of his car pulling out of the parking lot was a dying whisper.

She got through the Sunday dinner ritual with effort. She smiled mechanically at the antics of her teenage brothers. She trimmed Jennifer's shoulder length hair and Sarah's pixie bangs. By bedtime she was exhausted from pretending that everything was normal. She showered and changed into her favorite brown satin pajamas, but sleep eluded her.

Everyone else was sound asleep when she found her way to the front porch. The rocking chair creaked as she pushed it back and forth. The magnolia blossoms spread their fragrance through the cool night air, and she could hear the occasional call of a nocturnal bird.

It was time, finally, irrevocably, to face all of the past. She had allowed herself to remember some of her moments with Shane. There was still one memory that lingered, eclipsing the others completely. It was that memory that had left nothing but bitterness in its wake. It was that memory that she had buried until Shane's return.

Wendy stopped rocking and closed her eyes. Sleep would not come, but pictures of the past came easily.

Her junior year of high school had been a test of self-control. Finally her parents had given her permission to begin solo dating, and the boys had lined up at her front door for the privilege. She had waited eagerly for Shane to come home and ask her out. But relations between Shane and his father had become increasingly strained, and Shane stayed away. With each passing month, Wendy philosophically told herself that the older she was, the better her chances of receiving permission to date Shane when he finally came back.

Spring had arrived and with it an invitation to the high school senior prom. Wendy's date, Richard Franks, was the son of one of Gainesville's most influential commissioners. Wearing a robin's egg-blue chiffon formal that she had made herself, she was proudly escorted to the school gym that had been turned into a Polynesian fairyland for the evening.

It was while she was dancing her fifth dance that Wendy looked up to see Shane arrive. He was escorting a senior girl, Beverly Hansen, who had a reputation as tarnished as a silver tea service packed away in a widower's attic.

Wendy was simultaneously surprised and deflated to see him arrive. Beverly's father and Harnett Reynolds had common business interests, and it made sense that Shane would see Beverly socially. Still, to Wendy, who wanted Shane for her own, seeing the two of them together was a crushing blow.

Distracted, she let Richard lead her to the punch bowl. Still distracted, she did not notice that he was indulging in the local high school tradition of spiking their punch. The tasteless, potent 150 proof grain alcohol that he added to their cups made no impression on her as she sipped it. She was too busy watching Shane dance with Beverly.

Two cups later she was dancing again with Richard when Shane cut in. By then, she was beginning to feel the effects of the drinks, but it was easy to assume that her wooziness was because Shane's arms were around her, and they were drifting around the floor to a Carpenters' song.

"I didn't know you were home," she said softly.

"I got home today. Bringing Beverly was a last minute decision."

"You don't look as though it was too 'last minute.'" She leaned back and examined the sleek, formfitting navy tuxedo and ruffled shirt. She had to squint a little because her eyes weren't focusing quite right.

"I rented the last tux in my size. What do you think?"

She thought he was the best looking man she had ever seen. The local high school boys looked like awkward adolescents in comparison. "You'll do," she said, still a little hurt that he would invite Beverly to the dance.

"I didn't know you'd be here. Beverly called this morning. My father told her father I'd be coming in for the weekend." He pulled her a little closer, and she leaned against him, grateful for the support.

"That's how it's done?" she said as flippantly as she could manage. "Fathers send messages through fathers. I'll have to remember that."

"And what message would your father give me?"

"That I'm tired of waiting. I grew up and you didn't even notice."

"You've grown an inch and filled out in a few other places. Your hair is shorter, curlier if possible and you've had your ears pierced. That sweet little mouth of yours is softer, more kissable than it's ever been, and though you were never awkward, you have a new grace that takes my breath away. Are those the things I didn't notice, fairy child?"

His words dissolved her disappointment. "Then why didn't you call me?" she asked.

"Wendy, I don't trust myself around you. Ours is going to be a very short courtship, and you're too young for it to begin."

She was stunned. Shane held her tighter, and she could feel his aroused young body against her own. It was the most exciting thing that had ever happened to her. They drifted silently through three more dances before Wendy realized that her date had not claimed her again. "I should find Richard," she said finally, pulling away from Shane.

He let her go, and she found her date in the corner with Beverly. Reluctant to dance again after spending so much time in Shane's arms, Wendy accepted another glass of punch and then another. The night crept on. Richard and Beverly had developed a giggly camaraderie, and although Richard was still attentive to Wendy, she found herself dancing more with Shane than with him. It was when she began to stumble and giggle herself that Shane understood what had been going on.

The confrontation between Richard and Shane was volcanic. Shane insisted on taking both Wendy and Beverly home. Beverly refused to go, demanding to stay with Richard. In the end it was only Wendy that Shane led haltingly out into the school parking lot.

"I can't be drunk!" she had insisted, giggling uncontrollably. "Baptists don't drink!"

In the car she had leaned precariously until Shane had pulled her to his side to rest against him. The intimacy was slightly sobering, but not nearly enough. Wendy had never had any defenses against Shane to begin with. Alcohol and the heady realization that he wanted her loosened whatever inhibitions she would have had normally. She snuggled mindlessly against him, resting her head on his shoulder and her soft breasts against his chest. His response was a heartfelt groan.

She must have dozed because when she awoke they were at Shane's house. "I've never been here," she said, not finding it strange that he hadn't taken her home.

"If I take you home in your condition, your parents will never forgive me," Shane told her. "We're going inside. You're going to drink a quart of black coffee and sober up."

"Won't your father care?" She slid her hand up to Shane's neck and pulled his face to hers.

"He's not home. Wendy, behave yourself. We're going to be all alone in that house."

"Imagine being all alone," she said wistfully.

Shane shut his eyes momentarily and then pushed her gently away. "Watch yourself, fairy child," he warned. "I'm too young to be a saint."

"I love you just the way you are," she said and closed her eyes as the car door slammed.

Wendy's next memory was waking up on the sofa of Shane's living room with Shane kneeling in front of her, taking off her shoes. "This house needs a woman," she said softly as she took in the stark, masculine lines of the furniture. There were no adornments or accents of any kind. It was a shame because the house was wonderful, big and airy with high ceilings and ornate woodwork. "This house needs me." She had focused on Shane's face. "You need me."

He put his finger over her lips to silence her, but she kissed it, grasping his hand in hers to stroke her face against the callused fingertips. "Kiss me, Shane."

"Not until you sober up."

"Please?"

"You're playing with fire."

But she hadn't believed him. Wendy had known Shane all her life. She trusted him completely. There was nothing that could happen between them that could be wrong. It wasn't that she didn't understand what happened between a man and woman; it was just that, at that moment, those rules were meant for everyone else. She and Shane were exceptions in what was otherwise a strict moral code.

She had stretched her arms out to him in mute appeal. "Are you going to marry me, Shane?" she asked.

"Someday."

She watched his beloved face contort into lines of painful longing. "Then please kiss me."

But she was asking for more than a kiss, and both of them knew it. Weeks later, when her head was perfectly clear and loneliness and guilt had eaten away her natural serenity, she had tried to blame what happened on Shane and on the liquor she had inadvertently consumed. There was, however, no way of absolving her own part in their lovemaking. She had opened to Shane like a wildflower opening to the sun and the rain. Only at the last, when she was certain it was too late to stop, did conscious thought intrude.

She wept when it was over, as much for the beauty of having Shane's arms around her as for the pain he had caused and the guilt that quickly flooded her. She was stricken with remorse at the same time that she was thrilled with the realization that sometime during his passionate outpouring of emotion, Shane had told her that he loved her.

Shane had comforted her, his own remorse written on his features and audible in his voice. "I never meant for this to happen," he told her over and over again. "I didn't want to hurt you. You're too young for this."

But it had happened. Their immature bodies had reacted in a perfectly natural way to the immense attraction between them. When Wendy was calm enough to take a shower, she stood under the stinging spray and forced herself to be rational. She could not change what they had done. She had given something precious that should have been given later in her life. Brought up to believe that sex and marriage went hand in hand, she regretted the loss of control. But even though she and Shane were not married, she felt a commitment to him that she knew would never change. He had been her lifelong friend; now he was her lover. She had no doubts that as soon as possible, he would also become her husband. Her sixteen-year-old mind couldn't conceive of an unhappy ending.

Shane was waiting in the living room for her when she emerged. They sat on the edge of the sofa and tried to discuss what had just happened on that very spot. Products of strict upbringings and rural values, neither of them could say very much about what they were feeling. But when Shane finally took Wendy out to the car to drive her home, she understood that she was to wait for him and that when she had finished high school, he would ask her parents' permission to marry her. In the meantime he would see her as often as he could.

"But not alone," he said, as he pulled her close for a kiss meant to last them both for a long time. "I'm not enough of a man to resist you."

She had relaxed against him momentarily, a sign to them both that she would survive the night's encounter. Then she had opened the car door and gone into the house. It was the last time she had seen Shane Reynolds.

Now Shane was twenty-seven and undeniably a man. He was probably enough of a man to resist anything or insist on anything he wanted. And Wendy was a woman. She had grown up fast after their night together. She had grown up every time she walked to the mailbox to look for the letter from Shane that never arrived. She had grown up every weekend that he didn't come back home to see her. She had grown up the day she graduated from high school and knew that now Shane could marry her if he wanted to.

The night was starless black velvet, and even the crickets had stopped their chirping. Sitting on the dark front porch, it was easy to remember just how alone she had felt when she realized that Shane had not meant any of the things he had said to her. Slowly over the years she had forgiven herself for her indiscretion. But the experience had left its mark. She was no longer the innocent fairy child. She had lived with shattered trust, and sadly, it had changed her.

Now Wendy stood, ready to go back inside where sleep would finally claim her. Since Shane's arrival she had wasted time in reminiscences and regrets. Seeing him again had been the period to an unpunctuated sentence from her past. It was time to move on with her life.

Head held high, she closed the screen door quietly behind her.

Chapter Three

There were two truths that Helen Merritt, the owner of Melange, knew to be absolute. One was that people had a sacred duty to make something beautiful out of their world. The other was that she had been chosen to show them how to do it. Or at least she had been chosen to show the citizens of Hall County.

Other shop owners in the little city of Gainesville operated on the basis of profit and loss. Helen Merritt operated on the basis of her idealism and her own good taste. If she believed that an item should grace the homes of Gainesville's families, she stocked it, even if no one showed any interest in it at all.

"Someday," she'd tell Wendy. "Someday this will sell. Someone will come in, realize just what a marvelous piece it is and buy it immediately. It's my job to make sure it's here when they're ready for it." Consequently, Melange was an eclectic jumble of gift items, no small number of which showed signs of becoming permanent parts of the decor.

Late Wednesday morning Wendy unobtrusively held her breath as a young man and woman exclaimed over a three-foot glass statue of a rearing horse. The statue had been there longer than Wendy had, and Wendy had worked at Melange part-time for five years.

"It's wonderful," the woman said in tones of hushed reverence. "But it's a little more than we can afford."

"I was going to put it on sale next week," Wendy said, waiting for lightning to strike her dead. "I'll let you have it for the sale price." She named a figure that would have given Helen another heart attack.

The young couple left, horse in tow, and Wendy leaned against the counter with a Cheshire cat smile. She loved being in charge of the little gift shop. Situated in a Victorian house near the city's Green Street Historical District, Melange had a gracious Southern ambience that called to Wendy's own need for beauty. The four rooms downstairs were cluttered with china and glassware, silk flower arrangements and Irish lace, pewter and silver. There were less expensive items, too. Party ware in bright plastic, tastefully done stationery and greetings cards, colorful costume jewelry. Everything was designed to add beauty to a world much in need of it.

Now that Helen was staying in Clarkesville, Georgia with her oldest daughter while she recovered from her latest health problem, Wendy had free rein for the summer. Helen had turned the shop over to her, lock, stock and gift items, without so much as blinking an eye. Wendy suspected that Helen was thinking of opening a smaller version of Melange in the picturesque town of Clarkesville in order to be closer to her daughter. In the meantime, she trusted Wendy to keep Gainesville's Melange thriving.

Today, the shop was thriving with no one but Wendy to oversee it. The two young Brenau College students who normally helped part-time were both in other parts of Georgia for a week's vacation before summer session started. It had been a busy week, but that morning the skies had opened and poured inches of rain on the green landscape. The young couple who had bought the glass horse had been Wendy's only customers that day.

Gratefully Wendy had taken the opportunity to catch up on paperwork. Now it was almost lunchtime. Since the shop always closed on Wednesday afternoon, she gathered her account books and invoices and prepared to go home, but the chiming of the bell over the front door announced another brave soul who had ventured out into the miserable weather. Smoothing the skirt of her violet shirt-waist, she went to greet the new arrival.

Shane Reynolds stood in the small foyer, rain dripping from a dark-blue windbreaker. With automatic good manners he removed a cap that had protected his head. "Hello, Wendy."

His light-brown hair was damp and brushed back from his forehead. Raindrops glistened on his cheeks and in sparkling diamonds in his eyelashes. He wasn't smiling; there was a tense, expectant expression in his light-blue eyes.

Wendy didn't care what he wanted. She nodded without a smile. "Hello, Shane. I was just about to close for the day."

"Good. I came to take you to lunch."

He unzipped his windbreaker revealing a soft-blue Oxford cloth shirt that set off his bronzed skin. Carefully she moved a step back. She examined him, quietly wondering what kind of effect Shane would have had on her if they had not shared such an emotion-fraught past. The concept of sexual magnetism had never made sense to her. Why should one good-looking man appeal to her more than another? And yet, faced with the reality of Shane's presence, she had to give reluctant credibility to the concept of chemistry and its peculiar effects on the human species.

"Wendy?"

"I'm not going anywhere with you, Shane. I'm surprised you'd ask."

"Why?"

"Because I'm going home."

"No. Why are you surprised I'd ask? I told you we were going to talk." Shane stepped closer, and Wendy realized that if she moved away from him he would know just how threatened she felt. She stood her ground.

"But I don't want to talk to you." She kept her voice matter-of-fact. She had not graduated to pleasant conversation with him, but at least her words were controlled, with none of the revealing sarcasm of their last meeting.

Shane's smile was cynical. "Let's see. What was it you said to me in church on Sunday? Something about me not always being able to get what I want? In this case, it's going to apply to you. We're going to have that talk. You'll need an umbrella." He wrapped his fingers around Wendy's elbow as if to guide her to the door.

Wendy shook her arm, but his fingers remained firmly in place. Her memories of him, no matter how painful they were, did not include being manhandled. He had always been gentle even when he had held her in his arms that night so many years before. She turned to face him. "I'm not going anywhere with you."

"Then you'll force me to confront you in your own home."

He would do it, too. She didn't have a single doubt that he would do just that. He would pay a visit to her parents, and then, in front of them, he would ask her to go for a walk or a drive. And if she refused, she would be in the position of explaining her refusal to her family. "You're quite a manipulator, aren't you," she said with ice in her voice. "I'm surprised I didn't see it when I was sixteen."

"I'm tired of taking your insults." His voice was as ruthless as the bite of his fingers on her arm. "We'll have our talk, and then I'll leave you alone with your bitterness, fairy child."

"Don't call me that. Don't you dare call me that!" Shane's fingers loosened, and Wendy jerked her arm from his grasp.

Both of them were surprised at the sudden appearance of angry tears in her eyes. Wendy turned away to get control of herself. She had thought that reliving her memories would help her to put them aside. She had tried to close that chapter in her life, and for three days she had hardly thought about Shane Reynolds. But the scars were too deep; she had been a fool to think that she could take her memories out of storage, examine them and abolish their sting. She was Wendy MacDonald, and she had given her body, heart and soul to a man who had rejected them all. She could not be casual about something that had once meant everything to her. Not even if seven years had passed and she was no longer a heartsick adolescent.

"We'll talk, but we'll do it here," she said finally, turning back to face Shane. She gestured to one of the rooms behind her. "There's a sofa in there where we can sit. I have to close up first."

"You don't even want to be beholden to me for a meal, do you?" Shane shook his head as he examined her expressionless face. "Do you hate me so much, Wendy?"

"I don't hate you, Shane. But I have no appetite for either a meal or this conversation." Without a backward glance she began the process of closing down the little gift store.

The room where she had directed Shane was her last stop. While she pulled shades, secured the burglar alarm and locked up the more valuable items, she schooled herself to ignore him. His presence was incongruous in the lavender room that was decorated with mirrors and ferns, fine china and glassware. No matter what she now thought of Shane Reynolds, he was very much a man with an overpowering presence.

Finally, there was nothing left to do but sit beside him. The sofa was really just a love seat that Mrs. Merritt had installed for bored husbands. Wishing that she had chosen lunch instead of this enforced intimacy, Wendy sat next to Shane, carefully smoothing her skirt over her knees. She waited for him to begin.

"How long have you worked here?"

She had hoped he would get right to the point. Instead it was obvious that they were going to play a polite game and indulge in socially appropriate conversation. She pushed back her resentment and concentrated on remaining poised. She was still angry at herself for letting Shane see her emotions.

"About five years. I put myself through college by working here part-time during the school year and full-time in the summers. I also worked full-time for a year between junior college and Brenau."

"That sounds pretty ambitious."

Wendy shrugged slightly. "Necessary. No one was knocking down my door with scholarship offers. But between government loans and working, I managed."

"And now you're running the shop?"

"Just for the summer. Then I'm going to move to Atlanta and get a similar job there, if I can." She turned slightly so that she could see Shane's face. He showed no response to her words.

"Why Atlanta?"

She was fast tiring of small talk. "Why not?"

"I never thought you were a big-city girl."

"I'm sure you didn't." She thought about how incredibly naive she had been when Shane had seen her last. There was no question that her sheltered, rural background had been at least partly responsible for her foolish innocence.

"In fact I was sure you'd stay here, marry, raise a family."

"I told you on Sunday; no to all of the above."

She waited for more questions, but they weren't forthcoming. Twice in the same week she had been forced to endure the heat radiating from Shane's body as he sat close to her. She resented the intimacy as much as she resented the useless conversation, but she was powerless to put a quick end to either. With enforced calm she waited.

"I'll be happy to tell you what I've been doing."

Wendy heard the sarcasm, but she refused to apologize for her own disinterest. She remained silent.

"I graduated from the university and found a job south of Atlanta managing a cotton plantation."

"I knew where you were."

"I'm sure you did."

"News travels fast in this county. Even when you don't want to hear it."

Shane lifted an eyebrow. "But then you didn't need county gossip to tell you where I was, did you?"

The rhetorical question seemed to have meaning to him, but it held none for Wendy. She ignored it. "So, Shane. What shall we talk about now?"

Either he didn't want to get to the point, or he enjoyed keeping her guessing as to his intentions. He stood and wandered to the counter, examining the display of different patterns of china. "Do you enjoy this kind of work?"

"Yes."

"I remember when you were little. You'd be out in the woods playing with all the other kids, and then you'd see something, a stone, or an old branch, or some scrubby wildflowers. The next thing I knew you'd be gone, back to the house to make some sort of a decoration out of it." Shane picked up a small Dresden statue and then let out a low whistle when he saw the price. "These aren't exactly rocks and branches, are they?"

"And I'm not a little girl anymore."

"You weren't the last time I saw you, either." He set the statue back on the counter and turned to face her. "You were very much a young woman who knew what she wanted. Have you made me the villain all these years and forgotten what really happened that night?"

The sophistication Wendy had acquired in seven years did not fail her. Her voice didn't waver. "I have never pretended to myself that you were totally to blame. I threw myself at you, and you did what comes naturally."

"Then if you don't blame me—"

"I said I never felt you were totally to blame. I didn't say I don't blame you."

Shane nodded. "We were both at fault, but I was older. I should have known better."

"Is that what you came to say? Because, if I recall, you said the same thing that night. I don't need to hear it again."

Anger flickered across Shane's face, and Wendy could see that her own calm was affecting him. "You're so cool about all this. Cool and sophisticated. But you weren't so cool in the church parking lot, fairy child.''

She flinched at the nickname but refused to ask him yet again not to use it. He was doing it to shake her control. "Are we finished, Shane?"

"Not by a long shot." He picked up another figurine. "Tell me, who buys these?"

"People trying to make their environment more pleasant.''

He held the small figure of a shepherdess and caressed it slowly with his fingertips. He had farmer's hands, strong and wide. Wendy knew that his fingers would be callused from hard work. She remembered how they had felt caressing her.

"Yesterday I was carrying some of my father's things to the attic, and I opened an old trunk to store them in. It was filled with figurines just like these. Evidently my mother collected them. There were other trunks, too. One had doilies she had crocheted, another had Waterford crystal in it. My mother's whole life, consigned to the attic. All those years we could have had a part of her with us.''

If Shane had walked up and slapped her across the face, Wendy would not have been more surprised. He was sharing something amazingly intimate. Even his voice showed his longing. For a moment she forgot who he was and what they had once been to each other.

"Your father must have been in too much pain to keep reminders around him, Shane. Maybe he put the things in the attic for you to have someday when he was gone, too.''

Shane smiled a little. "Does that sound like Harnett Reynolds to you?"

"I never really knew your father."

"He was a hard man."

"My father says you broke his heart when you left town and never came back." She didn't add that she had felt a strong kinship to Mr. Reynolds since the same thing had happened to her.

"You and my father were the only ones who knew why I didn't come back."

His response was cryptic and puzzling. Wendy expressed her confusion. "Certainly I was the only one who knew what happened the night of the prom." Her voice hardened. "But I had to guess why you didn't come back just like everybody else did, Shane. Only I had more information to base my assumptions on."

Shane's eyes narrowed. "All the information in the world, fairy child. I laid it out for you, plain and straight."

She shook her head. "Did I miss something that night? The last thing you said to me was that you'd be coming back to marry me."

Shane's laugh was bitter. "I'll play the game. Tell me why you think I didn't come back for you."

"Because you had already gotten what you wanted." Wendy tried to be flippant, but her own pain was apparent in the words. She swallowed the sudden lump that was forming in her throat.

"Incredible." He moved closer and stood over her, glaring down at her. "You were young, but I thought you were more mature than that."

"Evidently you were wrong."

"Did you think I was making a collection of innocents that year? Did you think that after one night I was already tired of your sweet charms, so I decided to go on to greener pastures? How could you have misinterpreted—"

Wendy tilted her head to his and interrupted his words. "I'll tell you what I thought. I thought that you were a shallow young man who didn't know what an incredibly precious gift he'd been given."

"What a high value you put on virginity!"

She shut her eyes to block out his cynicism. "I was talking about my love."

Shane was silent. Wendy gathered her dignity like an invisible shield around her. "I'm going home," she said, opening her eyes but refusing to meet his. "We've both said too much. Seven years is a long time, Shane. There's nothing to be gained from discussing one mistake we made together."

It was as if her last comments had not been voiced. "Love?" he said softly. "If you loved me you would have let me know. All the guilt and regret in the world wouldn't have stopped you from writing me."

"And how would I have known where to write you?"

"From the return address on my letters."

Wendy noticed, for the first time, how hard the sofa was. She had sat on it a thousand times, but she had never noticed just how lumpy and uncomfortable it was. Nor had she noticed how loudly the ormolu clock on the counter ticked. She must check the thermostat, too. The room was suddenly, unbearably cold. Why hadn't she noticed the temperature before?

"Wendy?"

"What?"

"Why didn't you answer my letters?"

She had entered a still, waiting place. Her mind had ceased to function. She could only feel. She looked at Shane helplessly. His words were clear to her, but she could not form a response. "Letters?" It was the best she could do.

"That's right."

She was not a person who analyzed other people and tried to figure the motives for each of their actions. Now she found that she was too unskilled to begin to identify the purpose behind Shane's words. All she could conclude was that he was trying to ingratiate himself with a lie. She couldn't let him get away with it.

"There were no letters," she said in a flat voice.

"Of course there were."

"I walked to the mailbox for six weeks after you left. There were no letters."

"Not to your house, no. I sent them in care of Mary Lee Bennett because she was your best friend. I knew if I sent them directly to you, your parents would have questions about our relationship. I didn't want that to happen."

Wendy could feel Shane's eyes examining her. It was uncanny, really, that she could feel his gaze. Her own eyes were fixed on the wall straight in front of her. "There were no letters," she said in the same flat tone.

"You're calling me a liar."

For a moment she wondered how it would be to believe him. How would it be to pretend that Shane had cared about her, had tried to communicate with her? Would it change anything at all? It had been seven years. Neither of them was the same. Still, what would it be like to believe him?

"Liar is your word, Shane. I'm telling you what I know to be true. I never received a letter." She paused before she added, "Had you sent them, I would have gotten them."

"Perhaps you're the liar." She could hear the controlled fury in his voice. Each word was a sharp stone she could not dodge. She couldn't imagine why he would want to prolong this farce. She stood, but he blocked her path. "Were you so revolted by what happened between us that you decided to pretend it had never happened at all?"

"Yes, I was revolted," she said quietly, her eyes focused on a point right behind his left shoulder. "I was revolted that you took advantage of my innocence and left me alone after promising me everything. I was revolted that I gave myself to you with all the foolish love I had to give." She finally raised her eyes to his face and then to his own answering stare. "But I'm not revolted now, just tired of this discussion."

"I wrote you a dozen letters."

"Don't come barging back into my life armed with a pack of lies to smooth over seven years of silence." Wendy refused to move away although the fury in Shane's eyes was as threatening as a more physical response would have been.

"You don't want to hear the truth, do you? For whatever reason, you want to believe I left you without a backward glance."

Wendy knew that she should back off, turn around, find her umbrella and leave. But seven years of silence compelled her to tell Shane what she really thought of him.

"What I think is that you're a renegade, just like the people in town always said you were. You showed the moral strength of a fox in a henhouse when you left me alone. What if I'd become pregnant, Shane? Do you know what that would have done to my family? To my life?"

He stepped closer until there was no space between them. "Don't you think I worried about that? I thought that's why you didn't answer my letters, that maybe you were pregnant and your parents had forbidden you to communicate with me."

Wendy shook her head slowly. "There was no child."

"I found that out on my own. We were lucky."

There was no humor in Wendy's laugh. "Yes, we were, although at the time, all I wanted in the world was to have your baby someday. Imagine that."

"Wendy..." Shane's voice had softened as if the subject of their child had melted away his anger. He rested his hands on her shoulders. "I don't know why you didn't get my letters, but I intend to find out."

"Don't bother." She stepped back from him, shaking his hands away. "Don't try to cover up lies with lies. As far as I'm concerned, I'm done with dredging up the past. We've had our talk, now I'm going home."

"You're a hollow shell of what you once were. You're as hollow as one of those china figurines." Shane's voice was low, and the sadness in it cut through Wendy's defenses.

For the first time her voice shook. "You taught me well. One night in your arms was all it took. No one will ever hurt me again, Shane. I guess I should thank you for making me invulnerable."

"Don't thank me, fairy child. You're responsible for what you've become." He watched her face as he slowly zipped his windbreaker. "It's a small county. We'll be running into each other."

Wendy shrugged her shoulders.

Shane nodded and turned to disappear into the foyer. The bells over the front door tinkled, and Wendy was alone.

She had kept her body rigid throughout their discussion, and now she felt the strain in every muscle. She sought the comfort of the sofa and leaned her head against the back of it.

She waited for the surge of grateful relief that didn't come. It was over. It was finally over. There would be no more lies, no more recriminations. Even if they were thrown together again, there was nothing left to say. They were finally, irrevocably finished with each other.

But if that was true, why was there a persistent voice in her head that insisted she find out if Shane had been telling the truth today? If the past was really behind her, why did she have the overpowering feeling that by not trusting Shane, she was making another devastating mistake whose consequences might stretch further into the future than a mere seven years?

"You're still a sentimental fool, Wendy MacDonald," she murmured as she stared at the faint cracks in the ceiling. "But at least, this time, I'm going to stop you from acting like one."

Chapter Four

Although Mrs. MacDonald was genuinely sad that her children were growing up and leaving home, the children left behind did not mind the family's smaller size. Specifically they did not mind the fact that for once there was enough hot water to see them all through twenty-four hours. With careful time scheduling, each of them could shower without fear of ending with an ice-cold rinse.

Two weeks after her encounter with Shane, Wendy luxuriated in the plentiful hot water and planned her day. Since it was Wednesday, she only had to go to work for the morning. The leisure possibilities for the afternoon were tantalizing. She was torn between driving into Atlanta to research sections of the city for her eventual move and going to Lake Lanier Islands, a nearby recreation resort, with friends.

She had already been to Atlanta a number of times, narrowing down her choices on each trip. The city was full of interesting little neighborhoods of shops and houses.

She loved the bustle of downtown and the family atmosphere of the sprawling suburbs, but most of all she loved the in-between areas where other young professionals lived, shopped and generally enjoyed life. She wanted to live among them, sampling the best that the city had to offer.

Still undecided about her plans for the day, Wendy toweled herself dry and went to her room to choose something to wear. It was strange to have a room all to herself. She had shared it with Sandy and Stacey until they left home, and after three years it still felt empty without them. They had been her best friends. Even Mary Lee Bennett, her closest friend in high school, had not been as important to her.

She hadn't thought about Mary Lee for a long time, not until Shane insisted that he had mailed Wendy letters in care of her. Mary Lee had moved to Atlanta in the middle of their senior year in high school, and she and Wendy had hardly corresponded since. Wendy knew that M.L., as she had always been called, was married now with a small child.

It was insidious the way that Shane Reynolds still found ways into Wendy's life. She hadn't seen nor heard from him since the rainy morning at Melange, but the smallest things reminded her of his presence in Hall County. It wasn't unusual for the most innocuous train of thought to end up focused on him.

She pulled on a peach cotton sweater and a matching skirt with a geometric peach and cocoa pattern. She brushed her hair and then rumpled it with her fingers. A little makeup, peach stockings and brown leather pumps, and she was ready for work.

Breakfast at the MacDonald house was an every-man-for-himself affair, although that wasn't quite true because the MacDonald men were traditional enough to expect the MacDonald women to cook for them if they were available. In retaliation, the MacDonald women often delayed coming downstairs until the last disgruntled male had fried his eggs. The only exception was Mrs. MacDonald, who would cheerfully cook anything for the husband she adored. But even she drew the line at catering to her numerous sons.

This morning Wendy listened to the sounds of male voices in the kitchen before she entered. There were forks clanking against plates, and she knew that she was safe from having to defend her feminist rights. Obviously they were already eating.

"Good morning, everybody." Without waiting for a reply she headed to the stove for a cup of the coffee that would be in residence until lunchtime. "How is everyone today?" She poured her coffee and then leaned against the oven door to find out who was at the kitchen table.

"Good morning, honey," Mr. MacDonald said. "We have a guest for breakfast."

Wendy had discovered that bit of information for herself. Seated between her father and Jennifer was Shane Reynolds. Wendy concentrated on swallowing the steaming, bitter brew before she spoke. "Hello, Shane," she said as politely as she could manage.

He was dressed simply in blue jeans and a plaid sport shirt. He looked perfectly at home sitting at the table surrounded by MacDonalds. But then, he always had. "Hello, Wendy."

"Well, I'm off to work," she said, carefully setting the half-full cup on the counter beside the stove. "I've got some accounting to do before I open for business."

"You haven't had breakfast yet," Mr. MacDonald admonished her. "Make yourself something and join us."

"Is someone trying to get out of here without eating?" Eldora MacDonald bustled into the room, her expression merciless.

"I really need to go," Wendy tried again, aware that Shane's mouth was tilting in the direction of an unpleasant smile. She realized just how transparent she was being.

"Not without food in your stomach."

"When am I going to be old enough to decide if I'm hungry?" Wendy asked lightly, reaching for a box of cereal on top of the refrigerator.

"When I'm standing on the banks of the Jordan River waiting for the boatman," Mrs. MacDonald said, giving Wendy a quick hug before she poured herself a cup of coffee.

"I can see it now. After I move to Atlanta, every day at 7:00 A.M. I'm going to get a long-distance wake up call and a lecture on morning nutrition." Wendy poured the cereal into a yellow plastic bowl and covered it with milk. She had managed to avoid Shane's eyes during the entire exchange.

"Well, it's not every day we have such a nice guest," Mrs. MacDonald said with a warm smile for Shane. "Come sit down and enjoy him while he's here. You two used to be good friends."

There was no avoiding Shane unless she was willing to make a scene. Wendy conceded as gracefully as she could, taking the last seat at the small table. The next person wishing to sit down and eat would automatically have to go into the dining room and sit at the oversize wooden picnic table that could seat an army. She had been just a little too early.

"So Shane," Wendy said, knowing that some polite amenity was expected of her. "What brings you here this morning?"

She knew immediately that she had made an error. She should have asked something general. Instead her question had come out with a decidedly hostile edge. She realized that, quite simply, playing this game might be beyond her skills.

"Your father invited me."

"Shane's going to help me fix a tractor."

Wendy couldn't seem to help herself. "Can't James and Randy do it this weekend? They'll be home from the university, won't they?"

"You just wait until you see the twins, Shane," Mrs. MacDonald said, bringing the coffeepot to fill her husband's and Shane's cups. "They weren't even teenagers when you saw them last. Now they're grown men."

"They could probably fix it," Mr. MacDonald said, leaning back to watch his daughter with a lifted brow that she recognized as a warning. "But I need it right away."

"In exchange your father's going to come over to my place and help me evaluate the possibility of converting some of my land for organic farming." Shane was close enough so that Wendy could move her hand and brush the elbow he had propped on the table as he finished sipping his coffee. Her stomach tied into a knot around her hastily consumed Rice Krispies.

"Organic farming? It's about time somebody around here saw the light!" Jennifer's ears had perked up at Shane's statement. She was the family idealist, combining vegetarianism, health foods, yoga and meditation into a Northern Georgia version of a Southern California philosophy. The previous summer she had insisted on taking over the family vegetable plot and gardening without poison. Mr. MacDonald had finally had to intervene rather than watch the food that was to feed them through the winter disappear into bug tummies.

Shane grinned, and it was a grin that Wendy recognized. He hadn't smiled like that since he had reentered her life. It changed his face from solemn to glorious. He turned to Jennifer whose own face showed the rapt, unflinching attention of a religious disciple.

Jennifer, the last MacDonald daughter, was a composite of all her sisters. Her hair was the color of Stacey's, a warm honey-blond. Her eyes were Sandy's green, her mouth was Wendy's, small and kissable. And finally, she had gotten Sarah's myriad freckles. It was a charming combination with a potential for great beauty. Enthusiastic and intelligent, she had yet to give men more than a passing thought. Right before Wendy's eyes, that naiveté seemed to vanish into thin air. Her little sister was sure she had found a kindred spirit.

"Do you know anything about organic farming?" Shane asked Jennifer.

"I've read everything I could get my hands on. Everything! I've been trying to get Daddy to pay attention, but he'd rather murder bugs."

"Is that true, Raymond?" Shane teased Wendy's father. "Are you a certified bug assassin?"

Wendy watched the playful interchange that followed. As they discussed the land and the best ways to use it, she was struck by how easily Shane fit into all their lives. All but hers. Raymond and Eldora MacDonald were treating the younger man like a beloved son, and Jennifer MacDonald was treating him like the champion of all her causes. Sitting there, where he had sat many times before, Shane looked at peace, the natural tautness of his body relaxed and fluid. He looked at home.

"Now I really do have to run," Wendy said, standing and sliding her chair back. She didn't want to stay another minute and torture herself with the vision of life as she had imagined it when she was sixteen years old and full of dreams.

"I'll walk you to your car." Shane stood, too, and for a moment there were only the two of them in the kitchen.

Wendy was shocked at his audacity. "Don't bother," she said, sharply enunciating every syllable. There was an audible intake of breath from the kitchen sink where her mother was washing dishes. Wendy knew that she had given herself away. She tried to soften her words. "I know you and my father have work to do."

Mr. MacDonald's face was grim as he rose to stand next to Shane. "Yes. I'm ready if you are, Shane."

Shane's body had assumed its native tautness. Wendy was surprised at the remorse she felt for her own rudeness. "I'm going to drive into Atlanta this afternoon," she said into the silence. "Don't expect me for supper."

"Have a good time," Mrs. MacDonald said without her usual warmth. "I'll see you when you get home."

Wendy left, understanding her mother's parting comment for what it really was: a summons to explain her behavior when she finally came back. No matter what time she returned, Wendy knew that Eldora MacDonald would be waiting up to speak to her.

Wendy enjoyed the anonymity of the big city. At home, she lived closely with her family, and nothing was ever private. In the rural area of Hall County where she had always lived, houses might be separated by hundreds of acres, but neighbors, who were often relatives, still knew everything about one another. In Atlanta, Wendy had only a few casual acquaintances. Everyone lived his own life, and Wendy felt a sense of freedom foreign to her previous experiences.

There was so much to do in Atlanta: restaurants to try, stores to shop in, museums to visit. Little by little, Wendy was covering significant portions of the city. She knew that she would be happy living any number of places, but because she was forced to wait until the summer was over, she was taking her time and enjoying the exploration process.

Wednesday evening, after walking through the section of the city known as Little Five Points and eating dinner at Eat Your Vegetables, a restaurant Jennifer would have loved, Wendy wound her way to the interstate and made the drive back home. She drove slowly, thinking not about the punk style haircuts and wild clothing she had just seen, but about the coming interview with her mother.

Eldora MacDonald would not tolerate rudeness in any of her children. It was unheard of for a member of the MacDonald family to treat a guest with anything except the most courteous of manners. Wendy knew that her blatant hostility toward Shane that morning would not be overlooked.

Wendy was willing to take the dressing-down that awaited her at home. What she wasn't willing to do was explain her feelings about Shane Reynolds. In order to do that, she would have to tell her mother the entire history of their relationship. It was seven years too late to do that.

Wendy had often thought that she should have confided in her mother when she was sixteen. At the time, however, she had been unable to talk about it, afraid that her mother would turn against her for what she had done. Now she realized how wrong she had been. Eldora MacDonald's love was unquestioning and forgiving. But it was still seven years too late for confession. There was no reason for her mother to know, no reason for her to blame herself for not having guessed the truth.

Wendy pulled her little car in beside the family station wagon, opened the door and slid out slowly from behind the wheel. It was late enough so that the lights in the house were off except for one light in the living room. Theirs was an early-to-bed, early-to-rise household, and for a moment, she thought that she might have escaped the Georgia Inquisition. But as she neared the front porch she saw the shape of her mother's head, illuminated in the soft glow from the living-room window.

Eldora MacDonald was sitting in a porch rocker, and without a word she motioned for her daughter to sit beside her. Wendy sat and began to rock silently as she waited for her mother to begin.

"I never knew."

Wendy had expected to hear almost any other words. She couldn't think of a reply.

"I always suspected that somewhere along the way you'd had a bad experience with a man. I just never suspected that it was Shane Reynolds. You used to worship the ground he walked on."

"I used to be a fool."

Mrs. MacDonald took her time before she answered. "Perhaps not so much. Shane was a wild boy but a good one underneath all that bravado. No one ever loved him, at least not that he could remember. After his mother died, his father just withdrew from him. Shane has so much love built up inside him to give the right woman."

"I am not the right woman."

Mrs. MacDonald's rocker creaked slowly back and forth in the darkness. "Do you want to tell me about it?"

"Not now. It's too late."

"You must have been very young. Shane hasn't been back home in seven years."

"I know."

"Then he was very young, too. Yet you can't forgive him. That's not like you, Wendy. You've always seemed miles above pettiness. When everyone else was ready to tear down the house with their fights, you just sailed through it, oblivious to their human failings." Mrs. MacDonald stopped rocking and reached out to cover her daughter's arm with her hand. "Whatever happened, honey, you have to put it behind you."

"I did, years ago. But seeing Shane has brought it all back. I don't like being that vulnerable." Wendy stopped rocking, too. "Does that make sense?"

"I've always thought a trace of vulnerability would become you."

Her mother's words stung. "That sounds like a criticism."

"I'm not crazy about the impenetrable, sophisticated veneer you've been busily accumulating. Sometimes I wonder if my Wendy is still there underneath it."

Wendy drew in a sharp breath. She couldn't ever remember hearing such disapproval in her mother's voice. "That hurts," she said. "That hurts a lot."

"It was meant to."

The night was a dark curtain around them. Even the light shining through the window behind them failed to illuminate their expressions. What had been said, had best been said in the darkness. They sat silently waiting for the pain of giving and receiving criticism to begin to die away. When Mrs. MacDonald spoke again her voice alone betrayed her sadness at the necessity for this conversation.

"You're the most like me. Did you know that?" She didn't wait for an answer. "Sandy and Jennifer are their daddy's girls, and Sarah? Well, Sarah's not like anybody except Sarah." She paused as if trying to think how to express herself. "Stacey's like me in the way she loves children, but you're the most like me in the way you react to the world."

"I never thought of that." Wendy started rocking again and her mother took up the rhythm.

"Did you know that your daddy almost married somebody else?"

Wendy was taken aback. Like all the MacDonald children, she had assumed that her parents had been in love since birth. "No..."

Mrs. MacDonald laughed at the incredulity in the simple word. "It's true. I was blind-in-love with Raymond MacDonald from the time I was old enough to know what the word meant. And do you suppose he knew? I was a pesky younger sister to him. His daddy and mine were friends and when your grandpa would take me here, to your daddy's farm, I was sure I was in seventh heaven."

Wendy had heard some of this story, but evidently not all of it. "Where did the other woman come in?"

"Your daddy fell hook, line and sinker for the preacher's daughter. She was a prissy little thing who always kept her hands folded and her dress clean. I was ready to claw her eyes out when I discovered Raymond MacDonald was dating her. Then one Sunday they announced their engagement in church. I was sure I was going to die."

Wendy was dumbfounded. "Imagine!"

"Well, I didn't care if I lived or died. I couldn't even make myself be nice to either of them. But after the misery burned off, I started to get mad. I decided that if Raymond changed his mind and came after me instead, I'd never, never marry him."

"And?"

"And he did just that. The preacher's daughter was way too prim and proper for him. He broke their engagement and after a decent interval, he asked me for a date."

"Daddy always had good sense."

Mrs. MacDonald clucked her tongue. "But I didn't. I decided that if he didn't want me first, he couldn't have me last. I wouldn't go out with him. I was going to punish him for hurting me."

Suddenly Wendy could see the parallel. "Wait a minute—"

Mrs. MacDonald ignored her. "I almost lost him again. After I refused three dates your grandmother sat me down and told me in no uncertain terms that I was a fool. If I couldn't forgive your daddy for one mistake then I didn't deserve him anyway."

"It's not the same thing. I wish it were that easy."

"It wasn't easy for me, either. By the time I realized how stupid my pride had been, he was thoroughly disgusted. Then one night we were at a church pie party together. I had baked his favorite blackberry pie, and he wouldn't even bid on it. Just as another man was about to carry it away and me with it, I stepped down off the platform and stood in front of your daddy. 'Bid on that pie,' I told him 'or by gosh you'll be wearing it between your eyes.'"

If it had happened just that way, Wendy thought that it was the last time her mother had gotten that angry with the man she had been married to for more than thirty years. "And he bid on it?"

"Won it and me, too. But he wouldn't have if I hadn't been smart enough to forgive him."

"How old were you?"

"Seventeen. We were married a year later. I fell in love hard and quick, and it never changed. You're like me that way, too."

"I'm not in love with Shane Reynolds. Quite the contrary."

"I can hear myself saying the same thing about your father." Mrs. MacDonald imitated Wendy's tone. "I'm not in love with Raymond MacDonald." She patted her daughter's arm. "I don't know what happened between you and Shane, and frankly, I don't think I want to know. But I am sure that you're not going to be able to feel anything for anyone until you settle your differences with him." She stood and held out her hand to Wendy. "Think about it."

Wendy grasped her mother's hand and stood. "I'll miss you so much when I go to Atlanta."

"I'll miss you, too. I always hoped you'd settle closer than that. I don't like the idea of you being so far away."

Wendy smiled in the darkness. "Atlanta's not far. I can drive home in under two hours easy."

"But you won't." Mrs MacDonald squeezed her daughter's hand and then dropped it. "Just don't forget who you are, honey."

"I won't. If I can figure it out to begin with."

Later, when she thought about her conversation with her mother, Wendy began to understand one important piece of information. Eldora MacDonald suspected the level of involvement between Shane and her daughter, and yet, she had not condemned either of them for their youthful indiscretion. Had it been any other man, Wendy was certain that her mother's attitude would have been different. But Eldora and Raymond loved Shane like one of their sons. As a child and teenager, they had tried to give him the affection and guidance that he had desperately needed. Even now, in the face of Wendy's obvious animosity, they stood by him.

Wendy knew that Shane was often at the house during the day when she was at Melange. Her father was helping him analyze the potential of his land, and Shane, in exchange, was helping Raymond repair more of the farm equipment. It was a fair trade. None of the MacDonald men, except for the twins who were away most of the time, enjoyed tinkering with machinery. Shane did.

His name was mentioned frequently, mostly by Jennifer who had assigned Shane a place next to Ralph Nader in her affections. But because Shane was only there during the day, it was easy for Wendy to avoid actual contact with him until one evening two weeks after her talk with her mother.

It had been a hard day for Wendy. She had run a sale on some of the choicer items in the shop, and the result had been a barrage of customers. When six o'clock came and she could finally pull down the shades and lock the doors, she was exhausted. Nothing sounded better than a quiet evening and going to bed early. Instead, she arrived home to find a party in progress.

Mr. and Mrs. MacDonald had made a spontaneous decision to invite some of their neighbors over for a rib barbecue. Shane was one of the guests. He stood in a cluster of people with Jennifer by his side, and he looked perfectly at home as though he had never been away, never broken her heart.

It was a beautiful evening, clear and cool, with the promise of a lavish sunset. The MacDonalds no longer had any young children, but the neighbors had brought theirs, and pandemonium was only moments away. The ribs were almost cooked, sending their mouth-watering scent through the air to tantalize appetites, and gallons of Eldora's famous potato salad were sitting on ice for the big moment. Ordinarily, it would have been a special time for Wendy, who knew she would soon be too far away to indulge in such spur-of-the-moment country pleasures, but exhaustion and Shane's presence had wiped away her usual good spirits.

"You look tired, honey. Go change and then come on down for some supper." Eldora passed her daughter who was standing on the edge of the commotion trying to decide if she could escape unnoticed.

"I'd really like to go upstairs and go to bed. It's been quite a day."

"But that would be rude, wouldn't it?" Mrs. Mac-Donald was using her most persuasive tone, the one that struck fear in the hearts of all her children no matter how old they were.

Wendy smiled wanly. "Would it?"

"Yes."

With a shrug of her shoulders Wendy went into the house, carefully avoiding conversation with anyone else. She slipped out of her dress and into culottes and a knit tank top. When she could no longer avoid her explicit summons to dinner, she went downstairs to join the party.

At first, it was simple to ignore Shane. Enough people had been invited to make it easy to mill around without having to encounter him directly. Little by little, however, Wendy began to think that ignoring him was a bad idea. Jennifer had not left his side all evening. Wendy could see that her younger sister was completely enthralled with Shane's company. Wendy remembered, all too clearly, Shane's attractions for a girl Jennifer's age.

She began to watch them, collecting evidence to fuel her suspicions. Finally, when she saw Shane give her sister a brief hug before Jennifer moved off to join another group, Wendy's temper ignited. She was standing beside him in the space of a heartbeat. "May I speak to you, Shane?"

His smile was welcoming. "Hello, Wendy. I wondered if we'd have a chance to talk tonight." He excused himself from the group and took Wendy's arm. "Where shall we go?" he asked when they were a short distance from the edge of the crowd.

Wendy shook his hand off her arm and nodded in the direction of her mother's rose garden. Shane walked beside her, his longer legs keeping up easily with her determined stride. Once there she turned to face him. She wasted no words.

"Keep away from Jennifer, Shane. If you don't I'll tell my father about us, and I can guarantee that Raymond MacDonald is not liberated when it comes to his precious daughters!"

The expression on Shane's face as her meaning became clear was frightening in its intensity. He was a man who usually kept his emotions on a tight leash. At that moment he seemed to be a hairbreadth from losing control.

"Tell your father any damn thing you please! He's your father, but he's also a man. I'll tell him that once I made a very human mistake with his daughter, and that I tried and tried to rectify it, but she shut me out of her life. You underestimate Raymond if you think he wouldn't understand."

"Don't you touch my sister!" Wendy had only half listened to Shane's words in her determination to make her point.

Shane's hands settled on her shoulders like lead weights. "You little fool! She's only fifteen!"

Wendy bit off her words. "That's right. You like them a year older, don't you?"

His fingers were like claws digging into her shoulders. Wendy's head snapped back as he shook her in his fury. Her eyes were wide and startled. And sorry. She had not known that she could be so vicious in her own attack, nor that anything she said could ever provoke him to touch her this way.

"God, Wendy." His hands abandoned her shoulders and his arms closed around her as he pulled her to rest against his chest. "I'm sorry. I'm sorry."

"Shane..." Her voice was tentative.

"There's only one MacDonald woman I've ever wanted. Only one." The strain in his voice was without measure.

There were tears in Wendy's eyes, although she couldn't say if they were from anger, or pain, or contrition. She, who had always been above pettiness, had invented a new meaning for the word. She had known, all along, that Shane wasn't after her sister, and yet she had allowed herself to work up a fury over his innocent friendship with Jennifer. She had done it out of her own bitterness.

She raised her head to look at him, to tell him how sorry she was for trying to make trouble where no trouble existed. Their faces were inches apart. Up close she could see the web of fine lines that signified the seven years that had passed. His eyes were silver in the twilight, his skin burnished copper. He was memory, and reality, and all the things in between. He was Shane.

And when he lowered his mouth and sealed his lips gently to hers, she was only Wendy. The woman who had never for a moment stopped wanting him.

Chapter Five

I didn't plan that any more than I planned to shake you."
Shane dropped his hands and tried to step back, but
Wendy's arms were still around his waist. She didn't want
him to move away because once he did she'd have to erect
her defenses, veil the stunned expression in her eyes. She
held on, and in a moment he had gathered her close again.

"Wendy?"

"Why did you leave me, Shane? Tell me the truth."

She could feel him sigh. "After I took you home the
night of the prom, I went back to my house. My father had
come home in the meantime. He was supposed to be gone
for the weekend, but he returned a day early. While I was
taking you home, Beverly Hansen's father called mine. He
was furious. It seems Beverly had come home drunk with
her dress ripped, and she told her father that I was responsible for it. I guess she was afraid to tell him that she'd
switched dates and gone out on some deserted road with
the commissioner's son. Anyway, Mr. Hansen told my fa-

ther that if I wasn't out of town by the next morning he'd press charges."

"Oh, Shane." Wendy rested her head lightly against his chest. She was suddenly more tired than she had ever been in her life.

"My father found an evening purse on the floor by the sofa—your evening purse—but he thought it belonged to Beverly, and it was all the evidence he needed. I couldn't explain the truth to him because in my own mind the truth was much worse."

"And you left?"

"It was the last time I ever saw my father. Years later Beverly got up the gumption to tell him the real story. He wrote me a stiff formal letter telling me my name had been cleared, but he never asked me to come back home."

Wendy pulled away a little, and instantly Shane let her go. "Then it was my fault you lost your father. No wonder you didn't want to see me again."

"I never, for a moment, blamed it on you. I wrote you a dozen letters trying to explain why I couldn't come to see you right away. I knew eventually the whole thing would die down, and I could come back. I was going to confront Beverly and make her tell the truth, then I was going to marry you and live happily ever after." His voice trailed off, ending with a note of cynicism.

"I never got any letters."

"I know. And you don't think I ever wrote them."

Wendy saw steel in the silver depths of Shane's eyes. She wanted to believe him, knew that she must if anything good was ever to come out of their past. But she could not trust him. Too many years had passed, too many tears had been cried, too many new plans had been made. "I don't know what to believe," she said finally.

"Did you feel it, too?"

She knew what he was talking about, but she stalled. "Feel what?"

Shane shook his head. "Did you feel what was still between us when we kissed? Do you know how much I've wanted to forget you, how much I've wanted to condemn you for leaving your image imprinted on my life? But after all this time, whatever magic has always flowed between us is still there."

"Shane—"

He raised his finger to her lips, brushing them with his callused fingertip to silence her. "Nothing can grow between us again until you trust me. Nothing can root in the soil of suspicion."

"I don't know what to say."

"Then that's as good an answer as any, isn't it?" His finger found an errant white-gold curl, and he twisted it as his eyes studied her. "I almost got married last year. The daughter of the owner of the plantation I managed was more than willing, but I couldn't seem to make the commitment. And you, Wendy. You've sworn off marriage forever. What have we done to each other?"

Their eyes were locked. Each knew the truth. They would never be free.

Shane's finger caressed her cheek, then circled the rim of her ear pausing to worry her earlobe before he descended to her neck. "Don't," she said in a voice that said otherwise.

"You never said that to me before, did you? Tell me, fairy child. There must have been other men in your life by now. Are you satisfied without the magic we only hold for each other?"

"There hasn't been anyone special in my life since you left." Wendy raised her hand and stilled Shane's tracing finger.

Shane went on. "You're not the type to take lovers. You've been raised differently. What will that leave you?"

The sophisticated veneer her mother so disliked had been cracked into a million pieces. Wendy could only stare at Shane and wonder what the answer to his question really was.

"They'll miss us at the party," she said, finally. There seemed to be nothing more she could add.

"Then we'll go back." Shane turned and walked into the shadows. Wendy followed at a slower pace.

She knew he was watching her during the rest of the evening, and without her conscious permission, her eyes followed him, too. She drifted through the remainder of the party, a shell-shocked victim of her own emotions.

Wendy had no opportunity to act on her conversation with Shane. The next morning, her mother threw her back out of line and received strict orders from the doctor for two weeks of bed rest. Eldora MacDonald, who had never had more than an occasional cold, who indeed had never rested for more than twenty-four hours after the birth of one of her children, was forced to stay in bed and let Mother Nature work her healing magic.

Between Melange and helping with the additional chores at home, Wendy found no time to get away and little time to think. But as the weeks passed, she gradually came to the conclusion that she owed it to herself and to Shane to find out the truth. If he was lying, she needed to know in order to get on with her life. If he wasn't lying, she needed to know that, too.

There was only one way to test his story. Wendy knew Mary Lee's married name and the suburb of Atlanta she had moved to after her marriage. It had been years since they had really corresponded, but Wendy had received a Christmas card several years before.

On Thursday, Mrs. MacDonald, overly rested and as feisty as a hound dog on a leash, got out of bed, declared her back was healed and proceeded to take over part of her chores. By Saturday morning, she was back in control, shooing everyone away when they offered to help.

Wendy kissed her mother goodbye and set off for the city to find Mary Lee. It was a beautiful day, a day best spent doing something you loved, and Wendy resented having to spend it playing detective. Her life, which had been so orderly and goal oriented, was being thrown into chaos.

She was no longer certain that Shane wasn't telling the truth. Her heart and her head were evenly divided on the issue. She was not going to Atlanta to prove he was right, nor was she going to prove he was wrong. Mary Lee held the key to their past, and Wendy wanted her to relinquish it.

Outside of Atlanta, Wendy got on Interstate 285, circled the city and followed it to the Stone Mountain exit. She paid scant attention to the scenery or to the big granite mountain, which had a carving of three confederate generals on horseback, as she looked for a place to stop and examine a phone book. At a small café near the interstate, she pulled in, ordered iced tea and an egg salad sandwich and borrowed the Atlanta directory. Mary Lee had married Phillip Crane, and there were two Phillips and one P. Crane in the book. Only one of them was in the Stone Mountain area.

Wendy had debated calling M.L., although it would have been the simplest, most courteous way of handling the problem. But Wendy wasn't feeling courteous, nor did she think the matter could be handled efficiently over the telephone. She had not wanted to warn M.L. that she was coming and give her friend time to concoct excuses if excuses were necessary. Wendy finished her sandwich and tea and stood to make her call.

Minutes later she was following M.L.'s directions to her house. It had been years since they had communicated, but M.L. had not seemed surprised to hear from Wendy. Wendy wondered why as she followed the instructions, turning off a large avenue of fast-food restaurants and small shopping centers to the development where M.L. lived.

She parked her car on the street in front of a small brick ranch house with overgrown azaleas and one scrawny dogwood in the front yard. There was also a Sold sign on a post beside the lone tree, and Wendy knew that she had come just in time.

"Wendy!" The young woman waiting on the front step was plumper than Wendy remembered, but she had the same round face and luxuriant dark hair. Perched on M.L.'s hip was a smiling cherub with the pretty features of her mother.

"M.L.!" Wendy hesitated on the front step, wondering if under the circumstances a hug was in order. M.L. solved the problem by reaching her unoccupied arm out to Wendy, and the two former friends embraced.

"Come inside. I'm glad you called."

Wendy wondered if M.L. would feel that way in a few minutes. Quietly she followed her inside.

There were packing crates everywhere, some ready to go, some half-full. The two women picked their way across the living room and sat together on the sofa.

"Can I get you anything? Have you had lunch?" M.L. set her toddler down and then laughed ruefully as the little girl headed straight for a box of dishes. "I'll have to put her in the playpen, Wendy. I'll be right back."

She returned a few minutes later minus her daughter. "She's such a handful. Into everything."

They chatted for a few minutes about M.L.'s daughter, Candy, who was almost a year old, and about the move to Arizona that M.L. was looking forward to. Wendy accepted another glass of iced tea as she tried to think of a way to begin.

"I think I know why you're here," M.L. said as if she couldn't bear to continue watching Wendy try to find a way to bring up the subject.

"You do?"

M.L. nodded. "Shane was here about three weeks ago. I was just waiting for you to come. I'm glad you did."

Wendy watched her friend's face. M.L. had the contented look of a well-fed pussy cat. It was obvious that married life and motherhood agreed with her one hundred percent. But now, gazing at Wendy, there was a hint of sadness in her big brown eyes.

Wendy guessed the answer to her own question before she asked it. "Why was Shane here?"

"To talk about his letters."

"So it's true."

M.L. nodded, regret now clearly visible on her features.

Wendy leaned back and rested her head on the sofa. She had wondered for the past two weeks how she would feel when she learned the truth. She was still wondering. At that moment she only felt empty.

"I'd like to explain why I did it. It probably doesn't matter to you, but I'd like to tell you anyway."

Wendy managed a nod although she didn't yet trust herself to speak.

"Do you remember a boy named Warren Dantillon? He was in our class in school."

Wendy shook her head.

M.L. smiled a little. "That's amazing really. I remember everything about him, absolutely everything. I was so much in love that I'd have done anything for him. I almost died of sheer joy when he asked me to go out the first time."

Wendy was trying to remember. "Was he a short kid with a crooked nose?"

"That was Warren. On our second date I discovered that he was only trying to get in good with me because I was your best friend. I can't tell you what that did to me." M.L. stopped, and for a moment she sat in wistful silence. "Do you know it still hurts after all this time?"

"But I didn't like him. I hardly even knew he existed."

"You hardly knew anyone existed. All the boys wanted to date you, and you couldn't have cared less. When I found out Warren was one of the crowd, I wanted to get even with you. After the prom, I got my chance."

"You succeeded beyond your wildest expectations." Wendy tried to decide whether she should be polite or honest. Honesty won out. "It took me years to get over not hearing from Shane."

"'I'm sorry' doesn't cover it, does it?"

"Not even a little." Wendy searched M.L.'s eyes. "Did you have any idea what Shane meant to me?"

"No. If I had known I'd have hand delivered those letters within an hour of their arrival. Don't you see, Wendy? If I'd known you were serious about Shane, I couldn't have stayed angry about Warren. I would have realized you weren't leading him on. But I thought Shane was just one of the many guys in your life. Keeping the letters was silly and spiteful, but it wasn't malicious." M.L. reached out a hand and then let it drop abortively on the sofa between them.

"And you kept them all this time?"

"At first I kept them to gloat over."

Wendy lifted her eyebrow, and M.L. hastened on.

"I never read the letters, I just kept them and acted smug. Then we moved to Atlanta and I forgot I had them. Before I got married I went through all my stuff to move into this house, and I discovered that they were still in my possession. By then I was old enough to feel ashamed of what I'd done. I was so happy myself that I didn't want to think I'd ever caused you any unhappiness. So I invited you to the wedding. I was going to tell you then."

"I was working that day and I didn't come."

"No, you didn't. And I lost my courage. So much time had passed."

"A century."

"It's not too late." M.L. sat forward earnestly. "Shane must still care to have come all this way looking for me."

"It's been seven years! I'm not even the same person I was and neither is he. We didn't have a chance to grow together; we grew apart instead." Wendy pinched the bridge of her nose between her thumb and forefinger. For a moment she let anger and hurt rush in to fill the empty feeling that had come after Mary Lee's explanation.

"No, you're both different, but maybe that's okay. You were so young, Wendy. Now you're old enough to know what you want and need. You're old enough to know if Shane is the right man for you."

"Rationalizations, M.L.?" Wendy looked up at her friend, but M.L.'s expression was stoic.

"No, I know it sounds that way, but I think I have a point. I'm terribly sorry that this was forced on you, but since it was, I'm confident you can make something good out of it."

"I wish I had your confidence." Wendy stood. "If you still have the letters, I'd like to take them with me."

"Shane has them."

Wendy knew her own expression was incredulous. "If he had them he would have told me."

M.L. smiled another sad smile. "No. He took the letters because he knew I was moving out of state, but he wanted you to find me and ask about them. He told me you hadn't believed his story when he insisted that he had written you. I think he wanted you to trust him enough to find out the truth on your own."

A loud wail sounded from the other room. Candy's patience was all used up. M.L. stood, too.

The two women stared at each other. Finally, Wendy held out her hand. "What I'm feeling isn't forgiveness; it's shock. But forgiveness will come eventually and in case you're in Arizona when it does..."

M.L. took Wendy's hand. "I understand. I'm just glad you know."

"I guess I am, too." Wendy turned and wound her way between crates to the front door. She faced Mary Lee and managed a small smile. "Have a good life, M.L."

"Have a good life, Wendy. And if wishes can influence anything, know that mine are with you."

Wendy had the perfect opportunity to see more of Atlanta. It was still early enough to enjoy some of the city before she headed back home. But her thoughts and feelings were a tangled skein inside her that made it impossible to enjoy sightseeing. She wanted to talk to someone, but she had made a habit of not sharing herself with others. Since her sisters didn't know about her relationship

with Shane, there was no one she was close to who would
understand her feelings.

The trip home was mercifully quick. She left Stone
Mountain and returned home almost instantly, or so it
seemed in her preoccupied state of mind. Once there, she
pulled on an old pair of jeans and a hand-embroidered
work shirt that had been her teenage solution to looking
pretty while she did farm chores. Then she went downstairs and pleaded with her mother to give her a job to do.

Hard work had always been Eldora MacDonald's own
solution to life's problems. It was a solution she had passed
on to her children. One by one each of her older daughters had come to her when they were in the middle of a
crisis, and she had assigned them something to do to ease
the ache in their hearts. Eldora remembered Wendy coming to her once before. She had been sixteen, and her spurt
of activity had lasted for weeks.

"Well, it's not a very pretty job," Eldora told Wendy,
"but all the upstairs floors could use a waxing and I'm not
going to be able to get to it until I'm sure my back won't
give out again."

Wendy spent the rest of the day scrubbing, waxing and
polishing. She moved furniture with the determination of
an irate wrestler, letting the strain on her body begin to di-
lute some of the anger she felt at the trick life had played
on her. By the end of the afternoon the floors had never
looked shinier. Wendy had never looked more exhausted.

She showered before dinner and changed into a sundress with tiny stripes and a dropped waist. After the meal,
Mrs. MacDonald shooed Wendy out of the kitchen when
she tried to do the dishes. The time had come to face
Shane.

Wendy rolled the windows down in her little car, letting
the breeze ruffle her curls as she drove. She took the long

way to Shane's house extending what would have been a five minute drive into almost half an hour. By the time she arrived the sky was darkening. Wendy remembered the last twilight they had spent together and how Shane had kissed her. She remembered her own response and how easily he had knocked down her defenses. Tonight would be the same, for tonight there were few defenses to conquer.

She hadn't been to Shane's house, not even to drive by, since he had left town. The Reynolds farm was so large that the road it was on began and ended in front of Reynolds property. The house was set several acres back, behind a small grove of peach trees. It was a peaceful, gracious example of Southern architecture.

Wendy knew from her parents' gossip that Harnett Reynolds had come to Hall County as a young man to buy this farm, which had no house on it at the time. Land had been cheaper then, and he had worked hard to accumulate what he could, living in a one room trailer and getting by with next to nothing. By the time he married Shane's mother he was a wealthy man, and he had built this house, the largest in the immediate area, for her.

It was not a simple farmhouse. The design was two story and classic using cherry-colored brick and wide, white wood trim. There were fluted pillars on the small front porch and beautifully crafted shutters, which really closed, gracing every window. It was the skill with which the house had been built and the thought that had gone into each detail that made it such an outstanding success.

Over the years the house had begun to deteriorate. The trim needed painting; the shrubs needed a good trim. A poplar tree had fallen at the edge of the yard and still lay there, rotting. A long-neglected grape arbor was a tangle of twisted vines choking the life from each other.

The local opinion was that Shane's father had lost interest in living when his wife died, and that the house was tangible evidence. But even though it had been night when Wendy had been here before and she had not had a clear head, she was sure that the house had been in better condition then. Now she wondered if losing his son as well as his wife had finally pushed Harnett Reynolds into the depression that had made him lose all interest in the things he had once held dear.

She parked her car beside a Mazda and a new pickup, both of which she recognized as belonging to Shane. He was obviously home, and she was obviously going to have a chance to talk to him. What would she say? *I'm sorry I've despised you for seven years when I had no reason? I'm sorry I called you a liar? I'm sorry that life dealt us such an unfair blow, but now we can be friends again?*

Friends? They hadn't been friends since she was thirteen years old. They had been much more than that. Shane had been the stuff that fantasies were made of, and perhaps, she had been the same for him. He had been everything that adolescent girls dream about: handsome, wealthy, intelligent, gallant, dangerous. And she had been...what had she been? Innocent, spontaneous, charming, worshipful.

Now they were adults and there were no more fantasies. What could she say to him?

Her car door opened and a strong hand circled her arm. "Come inside, Wendy."

She slid from behind the wheel at Shane's urging. "I didn't hear you come up."

"You were lost in thought. I was afraid you were going to sit here all night." He dropped her arm and shoved his hands in the pockets of his jeans. She missed the warmth of his touch.

Wendy followed him up to the porch and inside. Once there, he guided her to a chair, but she refused, preferring to stand. The room was larger than she remembered it and emptier. Most of the furniture was gone.

"What happened to everything?" she asked, gesturing around her.

"I got rid of most of my father's things. I don't think this place had been cleaned since I left. There was very little I could salvage." Shane pushed his hair off his forehead only to have it fall once more to his brows. "We're going to get tired if we stand here and chitchat for the rest of the night."

Wendy realized how foolish she had been not to take the proffered seat. Now she was being forced to get right to the point.

The light in the room was dim. There were too few lamps for the wide expanse. In the shadows Shane's eyes seemed silver, as they had in her mother's rose garden. Silver and unreadable. Standing only a few feet apart, she realized just what a stranger he was to her now.

"It's not fair," she said softly. "We were cheated out of something important, weren't we?"

He didn't reply, and she knew he was waiting.

"I drove to Stone Mountain and saw Mary Lee today. I know the truth now."

"What was it our preacher always used to say at the end of his sermons? 'Ye shall know the truth, and the truth shall make you free?' Are you free now?" Shane's voice wasn't sarcastic; there was no discernible emotion in it. Wendy had no idea what his feelings were.

"I feel as though someone has peeled away seven layers of bitterness," she said. "But I don't feel free.... No, I don't feel free."

"Why not?"

"Because I've hurt you."

Shane didn't reply. Wendy knew that an apology was not enough just as Mary Lee's apology had not been enough for her. She could say the words, tell him how sad she was that she hadn't trusted him, hadn't believed him, but she knew it wouldn't even scratch the surface of his hurt. He was tense and unyielding. He had erected barriers that would not come down easily.

Without conscious decision she moved a step closer. She was close enough to touch him, to stroke the tight lines from his face. Tentatively she reached out to him. Her hand seemed to travel miles through the air before it settled on the firm, warm skin of his cheek. She brushed her fingers over his cheekbone, tracing the sharp angle slowly. He didn't blink at her touch, but she saw the quick exhalation of breath. He was not unmoved.

"Can you forgive me?" She heard the catch in her own voice, and she felt tears forming behind her eyelids. "I'm so very sorry."

"Are you?"

"Yes." Wendy felt Shane cover her exploring hand with his, felt his fingers lock with hers.

"And you believe that I never used you, never cast you aside?"

"Yes."

"Then the past is behind us." He moved closer, and his free hand tangled lightly in her hair. His face was still controlled, but his eyes were warmer. Blue, not silver.

Wendy relaxed at his words. They were a benediction. She smiled a watery smile. "Thank you."

"Do you know how much I've wanted to see some expression on your face other than distrust?" Shane smiled too. "I'd forgotten how beautiful you are when you smile."

Her breath caught, and she watched as he bent to kiss her. She could read in his eyes the kind of kiss it was going to be, even before his mouth had touched hers. It was meant to be a gentle kiss, similar to the one they had shared in the rose garden. And it started that way. His lips touched hers, stroking their softness with his own before he drew back as if to leave her.

The murmur of protest came from her own throat. It hadn't been enough. She didn't know what she wanted from him, but she did know that she wanted more than this. She swayed toward him, gripping his fingers in hers. Her other hand found his fine, silky hair and tunneled into it, as her lips found his mouth again.

Then there was no space between them. She recognized the feel of his body against hers. The kiss was familiar, too, heated and knowledgeable and very right. Her mouth opened against his and accepted his tongue's exploration. It wasn't enough, just as it hadn't been enough when she was sixteen. She understood again, as she had in the rose garden, how much she still wanted him.

This time when he moved away, her protest was more than a murmur. "Shane, don't go."

"What do you want from me, Wendy?" His question was without guile. She knew her answer could chart the course of their future. It brought her back to reality.

"I don't know." She let her hand slide down his neck before she reluctantly removed it. His hand left her hair; then their fingers were no longer entwined. They stood inches away from each other, strangers again.

"I didn't think that you knew." Shane stepped back. "For both our sakes, you'd better go."

Wendy nodded, turning to find her way to the front door. She needed the night air to cool her senses. On the porch she turned to tell Shane good-night.

"Wait here," he said. "I've got something that belongs to you." He returned in a minute, carrying a stack of letters fastened with a rubber band. Silently, he held them out to her.

She accepted them with a nod, not trusting herself to speak.

"Read them," Shane said. "Tonight."

Wendy nodded again. She touched his hand before she walked down the steps into the darkness.

Later that night she was grateful that she could be alone in her room. She had read and reread Shane's letters. She had cried helpless tears for the girl who had not known that she was loved and for the young man who had poured out his heart. She had raged at Mary Lee and then, finally, she had let forgiveness fill her heart. Now she sat by the window gazing at the moonlit landscape. And she knew that five miles away, Shane was probably doing the same.

Chapter Six

Y ou're probably the only person in the world who makes ham sandwiches like she's working on an assembly line.'' Wendy watched Sarah methodically slap mustard on twenty pieces of bread, then start all over with mayonnaise.

"And you're the only person in the world who thinks that people would rather eat a radish that looks like a rose than a radish that looks like a radish."

Wendy continued to trim and slice the vegetables for the relish tray that was beginning to look as if it belonged in an exhibition of edible art. "How do you suppose Ma handled making meals for all of us? With almost everyone coming back for the holiday, I'm beginning to get a feel for what it must have been like."

"She developed shortcuts, and she loved what she did."

"I've never seen her happier. With Stacey and Sandy both coming and bringing the grandchildren, Ma's in seventh heaven." Wendy offered a radish to Sarah. "It'll be good to see them. The Fourth of July wouldn't be the same without little kids to enjoy the display."

Sarah waved the radish away. "Remember the year we almost burned down the barn with the Roman candles that Thomas got hold of somewhere?"

"They belonged to Shane." Wendy stood and stretched. "If Thomas was in trouble, you could always count on Shane being in the background somewhere."

"You're not angry at Shane anymore, are you?" Sarah's question was casual. She was busily covering the bread with slices of ham.

"No, I'm not. Observant, aren't you?"

"It doesn't take any great psychic powers to put two and two together." Sarah began on the cheese. "I've never seen you so rattled before. It's been . . . interesting."

"I'm glad it was interesting for someone."

"Are you in love with him?"

"Sarah!"

Sarah swept her sister with her unusual golden eyes. Of all the MacDonald girls, she was the only one who couldn't be considered pretty in the traditional sense. Her heart shaped face was framed by short shining brown hair that emphasized high cheekbones and a delicate nose. It was an arresting face that people always looked at twice although they were often unsure why. Right now it was a face filled with perception. "I thought you were the one who was never going to fall in love, never going to marry."

"You're imagining things."

"No, I distinctly remember you saying that you weren't going to fall in love, weren't going—"

Wendy dropped her knife on the floor and bent to retrieve it. "No, I meant you were imagining things about my relationship with Shane."

"I don't think so." For just a moment there was a trace of vulnerability in Sarah's voice. "But if you don't want to tell me, that's okay."

It really wasn't, and Wendy understood that she had hurt Sarah. There were three years between them, and Wendy had always aligned herself with her two older sisters. She had never realized that Sarah felt left out. Unflappable Sarah with the photographic memory and the sensible approach to living wanted to be included in Wendy's life.

"I did love Shane once," Wendy said quietly. "Nobody but Ma knows it, Sarah."

Sarah's eyes softened. She realized that Wendy had just given her a special gift. "When the two of you are within fifty feet of each other, sparks fly. It's like the Fourth of July every time."

"Then I guess it's a good thing we rarely see each other, or we might set something on fire." Wendy tried to say the words lightly, but she couldn't. She missed Shane. They had avoided each other since the night she had apologized for not believing that he had written her. Wendy wondered if Shane was as much at a loss for words as she was.

"You'll be seeing him today. He's been invited to spend the afternoon here."

Wendy looked down at the shorts and shirt that had seemed perfectly appropriate not more than thirty seconds before. She stood. "Well, I'm all done with the relish tray." She dumped the rest of the untrimmed radishes in the middle, destroying her design entirely. "I think I'll run change my clothes before Sandy and Stacey get here."

Sarah nodded without even a trace of a smile. "That sounds like a good idea." She watched Wendy disappear through the doorway, and then with obvious distaste picked up a knife and began to carve the radishes herself.

Sandy and her family arrived at the MacDonald farm first. They lived in the small city of Cameron, Georgia, about one hundred miles away. Tyler was a well-known lawyer with a busy practice, and Sandy had spent the past year finishing up law school at the University of Georgia and giving birth to their first child, Bonnie Charlotte Hamilton. With their hectic schedule, no one had seen nearly as much of them as they would have liked. When they pulled up in their new station wagon, the whole MacDonald clan went wild.

Wendy patiently waited her turn. She was Bonnie's godmother, which was a measure of the closeness between Sandy and herself, and she wanted a chance to cuddle her new niece and hug her sister. First, however, she was handed to Tyler for a warm and thorough embrace. Wendy had never had any difficulty understanding Sandy's attraction to Tyler Hamilton. A dignified man from an old Georgia family, Tyler had stepped into her sister's life and changed it forever. Wendy had watched the changes occurring, applauding some, worrying about others. Now, however, Tyler and Sandy had settled down into a give-and-take that was marriage at its very best. Sometimes it made Wendy wonder about her own life plans.

"Wendy!" Sandy grabbed her sister with one arm and pulled her close. "It's been so long!" Sandy shifted the bundle in the light blanket and handed it to Wendy. "What do you think?"

Wendy looked down at her four-month-old niece. Bonnie's eyes were focused on her aunt and she was smiling happily. "Aren't you beautiful!" Wendy wrapped both arms around the baby and lifted her higher. "Aren't you something?"

"I think she looks like you," Sandy said. "Her eyes are blue like Tyler's, but I could swear she's going to have your mouth. And if she ever gets any hair, I just know it's going to be curly."

Wendy grinned, examining Bonnie carefully. "I think you're right. How thoughtful of you." Reluctantly she passed the baby on to Sarah and Jennifer who were waiting their turns. "She's grown so much in three months. And you're looking great. Motherhood agrees with you."

"So does working with Tyler. I just pack Bonnie up and take her to the office with me a couple of times a week. I have two cases I'm working on."

"What do you do when you're actually with your clients?" Wendy pictured Sandy burping the baby as she talked about divorce settlements and property disputes.

"Tyler takes her. Actually, I have to fight him for her whenever I'm there. The man's crazy about his little girl."

Tyler had come up to stand beside them. "And his big one," he said. Wendy caught the look that passed between husband and wife. For a moment she imagined Shane looking at her just that way.

The Hamiltons settled into the chaos happily. An hour later the Cunningham family arrived driving the blue van that had taken them on many a camping trip. Stacey had married Ryan and become an instant mother to his four orphaned nieces and nephews. Now, four years later, Stacey and Ryan had a three-year-old boy of their own, Devin, and another baby on the way. As Stacey stepped out of the van, magnificently pregnant, Wendy thought she had never looked happier.

The MacDonald women served gallons of iced tea and lemonade and Sarah's sandwiches. Wendy was so caught up in the conversation around her that she forgot to think about Shane's arrival. At least that was true unless she intercepted the affectionate byplay between Stacey and Ryan, and Sandy and Tyler. Her two older sisters had married men who thought the sun rose and set with them. What would it be like to have someone feel that way about her?

"Stacey, Sandy, do you remember Shane Reynolds?"

Wendy looked up to see Shane standing on the porch steps beside her father.

Stacey stood, a welcoming smile for Shane. "We went through school together. Of course I remember. Come meet my family."

Wendy stood on the edge of the porch watching the friendly introductions. Against her will she noted how well Shane fit in with her two brothers-in-law. He was a success in his own field, just as they were in theirs. All three of the men gave the impression of quiet strength. Shane was younger than either Ryan or Tyler, but he carried himself with the same dignity and self-confidence. With Shane, though, there was something more: a certain wildness underneath the surface, a certain vulnerability.

Wendy caught Shane's eye as the last thought occurred to her. She had never considered him vulnerable before, and yet it was plainly visible to her now. There was a lull in the introductions, and he turned to face her. She understood that whatever she did would determine the shape of their relationship. With her eyes still locked with his, Wendy extended both hands to him.

"Hello, Shane."

He gripped her hands in his, and then, as if to seal his claim, he bent and kissed her cheek, his mouth lingering at the corner of hers. "Hello, Wendy."

She wanted more, just as she always wanted more when he was near. But she also realized that just by having as much as she had, she had alerted the MacDonalds to the nature of her relationship with this man. She was not casually affectionate. In public she might kiss or hug her own family, but as popular as she had been in high school and college, she knew and her family knew that she had still been considered standoffish by the young men who wanted more than she would give.

Somehow, she didn't care. Still holding Shane's hand, she pulled him to stand beside her. She did not want to let him go, not even to keep her feelings secret. "I'm glad you're here," she said, wondering how anything could be such an understatement.

"So am I."

They both knew that seven years had passed, but with the bitterness between them gone, Wendy could almost pretend that time had stood still. Shane helped her clear plates and glasses off the front porch and they chatted together at the sink as she washed and he dried the dishes. The kitchen was a busy thoroughfare and they couldn't talk about anything intimate, but they reminisced about other Independence Days and told each other stories about Wendy's brothers and sisters.

Afterward, they strolled hand in hand to the pond with Sandy and Tyler and Stacey's two youngest children and taught the little ones to feed dog food to Mr. Mac-Donald's gigantic catfish. At the woods, Wendy and Shane parted from the others, striking off on their own.

They wandered without speaking as they enjoyed the shade of the big trees and the poignancy of the moment. Finally Shane stopped and leaned against the trunk of an oak. He pulled Wendy to rest against him, cradling her between his thighs. She shut her eyes as his hands traveled the length of her back and settled at her waist.

"I never forgot the way you felt in my arms."

She opened her eyes, suddenly shy but not wanting him to know. Whatever sophistication she had garnered did not cover this situation. "I never forgot, either."

"You were so beautiful, so giving. When I felt you against me, I thought I'd die from it."

"Shane..."

"I would have died before I hurt you."

She focused her eyes on his collarbone. "It's all over now."

"Is it? I still want you in my arms. You're still the same beautiful, giving woman."

"But I'm not." She lifted her head slightly. "I wasn't a woman then. Not at all."

"You became a woman in my arms."

She tried to smile. "That's a very old-fashioned sentiment. If it's true, I wasn't ready for it."

One of his hands found her chin and lifted it so that her eyes could no longer avoid his. "That's what I'm sorriest about. You say you'll never marry. Is it because of what happened? Did it scare you so that you'll never want another man?"

Wendy saw the deep regret in his eyes. "No," she said softly. "It was what happened afterward that scared me. I felt so guilty and so alone. I thought I'd given my trust to the wrong man. And Shane, if I couldn't trust you, I didn't think I could ever trust anyone again."

"And now?"

"Now I know that I didn't make a mistake, that you felt exactly as I hoped you did."

"Where does that leave us?"

"Seven years older."

"And seven years hungrier." His legs closed around her, holding her in place, and his hands sought her curls, threading his fingers through them as he brought her mouth to his. This time gentleness wasn't enough. His lips were fierce and wild against hers, telling her of his hunger and of his regrets. Wendy pressed against him, knowing as she did the strength of his arousal and the undeniable response of her own body. His tongue swept her lips, and she opened for the full glory of his kiss. His taste and touch and smell were all familiar, blending with memory, more than memory, much, much more.

"In seven years, there was nothing I wanted as much as this," Shane whispered, his mouth at her ear.

"I'd wake up at night sometimes, dreaming that you were kissing me." Wendy leaned against him, her hands on his shoulders. "And I'd hate myself for dreaming."

"It's not too late."

Warning bells sounded in Wendy's head. "Neither of us knows if that's true."

"You can't tell me you don't feel what's still between us." Shane's arms tightened around her. "You're melting against me, fairy child."

"But that's not enough, is it?"

"It's enough for now. I'll take what I can get."

"But I don't know how I feel, what I can give you. We're different people."

"Different people who don't want each other any less." His mouth closed over hers again, cutting off the murmured protest in her throat. This time, his hands caressed her back as his tongue played with hers. His touch was light, a whisper, that did nothing to lessen the ache building inside her. Wendy had been kissed by enough men to recognize an expert. Whatever else Shane had done in seven years, he had found the time to practice his already well-honed skills.

"How many women have you kissed like that since you last kissed me?"

Shane smiled at the petulance in her tone. "Enough to tell the difference between them and you."

"And what is the difference?"

"I love you."

The words were said so casually that for a moment their importance was lost to her. She wrinkled her forehead as she tried to put them in perspective.

Shane continued. "Don't tell me you didn't know. You read the letters."

"They were written a long time ago. Shane, how can you still love me after all this time?" Wendy's forehead was still wrinkled, and Shane lifted his hand to smooth away the worry lines.

"What did you think this was all about? Did you think I came back to open up old wounds for the fun of it?"

"Why did you come back?"

"To marry you."

Wendy slumped against him and then realized that the even more intimate posture was a mistake. But when she tried to pull back to a safer distance, Shane wouldn't let her. "As far as you knew, I was already married," she said, her head on his chest.

"I haven't been honest about that. I've kept up with you, fairy child."

There was a short silence as she processed this new piece of information. "Why didn't you just come back and face me years ago then?"

"Don't forget, I didn't know why you refused to answer my letters. When I got over being hurt, myself—and that took years—I decided that we needed time and distance between us. I thought that's what it would take for both of us to grow up and put everything in perspective."

"And if I'd found another man in the meantime?"

"I would have been back in an instant to claim you myself."

"And you think I would have just melted in your arms!"

"Like you're doing now? The thought did cross my mind."

Wendy stiffened, but the humor of the situation took precedence over righteous anger, and without her permission a throaty giggle escaped.

"Ah, Wendy, it's been so long since I've heard you laugh. Do it again."

She shook her head, refusing to let him off that easily.

"Let's see if I remember how to make you." Shane's hands traveled the length of her back again, settling at her waist and slowly inching up her rib cage. His fingers fluttered gently as he went. "Back in the days when Thomas and I thought girls were just for tormenting, he taught me to be a master at this."

"Thomas never taught you that!" Wendy gasped. "He only tickled bare feet."

"You're right, maybe this wasn't Thomas after all. Now that I think about it, it was probably Beverly Han—ouch!"

Wendy had kicked him, ineffectually landing a puny blow on Shane's boot with the toe of her sandal. She was sure he hadn't even felt it, but he dropped his hands in mock agony. She backed away, noting the feral gleam in his eye as he stopped pretending he was hurt and began to stalk her instead.

"Now I can't let you get away with that kind of abuse, Wendy. What would Thomas say?"

"Thomas lives in Washington state. He'll never know." She backed away, an uncontrollable grin wreathing her features. She was transported back to her childhood. Al-

most. Actually the game had never been this exciting, this
dangerous when she was six and Shane was ten. With a
delighted laugh that was as big as the forest surrounding
them, she turned and began to run.

They wove in and out of the trees, Shane just a step behind her. Both knew that if he wanted to catch her it would
be easy. His legs were longer, his body more accustomed
to physical exertion. And Wendy couldn't seem to stop
laughing, which greatly hampered her speed. Seven years
worth of suppressed joy bubbled up inside her, easily pen-
etrating the sophisticated mask she had worn to protect
herself. It was summer, and the sun shone brightly through
the trees, dappling the ground as she ran. Most of the
people she loved best were a stone's throw away. And
Shane? Shane, the only man she had ever loved, was right
behind her.

She stopped suddenly and turned with her arms out-
stretched. He pretended to stumble against her, and then
they were lying on a bed of pine needles together. Wendy
pulled his head down to hers and wrapped her arms around
his back. They kissed, pausing only to breathe and laugh
again. It was only when he began to untie the cord that
laced the two halves of the front of her sundress, that
reality intruded.

Wendy lay wide-eyed in the shade of the pine trees as he
loosened the cord. His eyes held hers as his fingers gently
brushed the soft, smooth skin of her neck and then dipped
lower to the tops of her breasts. Then his mouth followed
the path of his fingers. He was creating his own fireworks
display, each touch of his lips was a fierce explosion inside her, and she couldn't find the words to stop him.

He was so dear, this man who could ignite a conflagra-
tion inside her without half trying. She had loved him so
long and so well, and if that had changed, the enormous

physical attraction between them had not. She wanted him more than she ever had before, for now she was old enough to know what wanting could lead to. And this time she knew it would be sensual magic between them.

He stopped, resting his head on her still-clothed breasts, and Wendy stroked trembling fingers through his fine, silky hair. She wondered if she would have had the strength to resist him if he had made further demands. She was beginning to understand some new, disconcerting things about herself. One of them was that Shane held a power over her that no other human being had ever held.

He seemed to be able to read her mind. "I'm not going to push you into anything you're not ready for. I grew up, too."

Suddenly it all seemed so unfair. "I wish you'd sent those letters to me!" she said.

"What you wish is that we'd married when you were fresh out of high school and so crazy in love with me that no other possibility entered your mind."

"We'd probably have a child by now." Wendy heard the longing in her own voice.

"Would you have been happy?"

"I think so."

"You can still have it then. I'll marry you in a moment, give you a child on our honeymoon."

She continued to stroke Shane's hair. "Is that what you really want?"

He rolled to one side and propped himself up on an elbow to watch her as they talked. "Are you ready to hear what I want?"

She faced him, propped on an elbow, too. They were close but no longer touching. Shane's gaze flickered to the still untied bodice of her dress, and with one hand he pulled the cord tighter. He smiled at the rush of color in her cheeks.

"I want the family I never had," he said quietly. "It doesn't have to be larger than life like the crazy Mac-Donald household, but I want to come back to my house at night to the woman I love and to children I'd lay down my life for. I want to work my land and know that I'm working it for them, and that someday they'll be working it for their children. That's all I want."

"You sound like my father."

"But I'm not your father."

Wendy tried to smile. "You certainly aren't. But Shane, this is all happening too fast for me."

"I know. You have different dreams." Shane's tone was careful, nonjudgmental.

"I've never been away from home. I couldn't even go away for college. I've just been waiting to see some of the world. Can you understand that?"

"I've seen the world. There's nothing there that you can't find in your own backyard."

"Not for you. But it might be different for me. I've had a home and love and family. I want something more." She raised her hand to touch his hair. "That doesn't mean I don't want you, don't care about you...."

"Don't love me?"

Wendy shook her head. "I don't know."

Shane lay back against the pinestraw, an arm flung over his eyes to protect himself from more than the sun. "I told you I'm not going to push, Wendy. I meant it."

Wendy wondered what peculiar trick of chemistry it was that made her want to throw herself at him and tell him he could have everything he wanted, even her dreams. Instead she took a deep breath and sat up. "I think we should go back now. My family will be looking for us. Especially my father."

"Your father must have been quite a young man himself to worry so much about his daughters' suitors."

It was just the light touch they needed to temporarily banish the tension between them. Wendy extended her hand and pulled Shane up to sit beside her. He leaned over and kissed her nose before he stood. "Better let me brush the pine needles off your back, or there'll be a shotgun wedding to cap off the Fourth of July."

She did as she was told, following his ministrations with her own, then hand in hand they walked back to the house.

Wendy often wondered what people who lived up north substituted for front porches. It seemed to her that some of the most important moments of her life had been spent sitting in a rocking chair with the cool evening air drifting around her. That night, as she rocked slowly back and forth listening to the sound of a mockingbird in the magnolia tree, she wondered idly if she could find an apartment with a porch in Atlanta.

It had been the most wonderful Fourth of July she could remember. Shane had stayed until late, eating his share of the dozens of chickens that had been barbecued and the mountain of coleslaw and baked beans. He had helped Stacey's twin sons set off Roman candles without burning down the barn, and he had joined in the after supper sing that had lasted until the children had fallen asleep in their parents' and grandparents' laps. Then, before leaving, he had pulled Wendy into the shadows to kiss her good-night. Their discretion hadn't fooled anyone; the word was out. Both Stacey and Sandy had cornered her to point out that they had known, all these years, that Wendy had once had a serious crush on Shane. Nothing she could say would dissuade them.

It had almost been too perfect. Too achingly familiar and perfect. She had always loved these family gatherings, but never more than today with Shane by her side showing her the same courtesies that Ryan showed Stacey and Tyler showed Sandy. It was a scene from her childhood fantasies, and she understood that it was a scene from his, too. Shane, who had never had a family life of his own, had found total acceptance in the MacDonald clan.

There was so much to think about that she couldn't think about any of it. She rocked as if the confusion of her feelings would somehow dissipate with the gentle back and forth motion.

"Wendy?"

Sandy stood in the doorway, her long golden hair an effective robe around the floor-length nightgown she was wearing. Bonnie was draped casually over her shoulder. "Can I join you?"

"Of course. Is Bonnie hungry?"

"The correct question is: 'is Bonnie hungrier?' She's always hungry." Sandy sat in the rocker beside Wendy and unbuttoned her gown. In a moment Bonnie was sucking happily. "I didn't want to wake Tyler. He looked so peaceful."

"Does it bother him when you nurse her in bed?"

"He likes to watch. He wanted a child for so long, he likes to be part of all of it."

"The elegant Tyler Hamilton is an unabashedly enthusiastic father. It's beautiful to see."

"It is, isn't it?" Sandy looked up and smiled at Wendy. "You know what else is beautiful to see? The way Shane Reynolds looks at you."

It was too late at night to pretend. "Shane says he loves me."

"And what will loving him do to your plans to go to Atlanta?"

"I didn't say I loved him."

Sandy propped Bonnie's head a little higher, patting her bottom affectionately as she did. "You know, there's always been a mystery about you. You told me once that you'd been in love in high school, and at the time I was too upset about my own problems to pay much attention. But I'm guessing now that the boy you loved was Shane." Sandy looked up and her eyes locked with Wendy's. "If you don't think you're still in love with him, you're fooling yourself but no one else."

Wendy didn't even realize that her head was shaking back and forth. "I can't be in love. Not with Shane, not with a man who's so thoroughly tied to the soil."

"And I didn't think I could fall in love with a distinguished lawyer from one of the South's finest families. Love has a habit of choosing blindly."

Wendy watched silently as Sandy put Bonnie over her shoulder and patted her before switching her to the other breast. Bonnie was well settled before Wendy answered. "You and Stacey both would have been perfectly content to live your lives down that dirt road out there. I'm not."

"And will you be content to live it without Shane's arms around you?" Sandy looked down at the baby nestled against her. "She's fallen asleep." Gently she dislodged her sleeping daughter and held her against her shoulder, standing as she did. "Wendy, I wish things could be simpler for you. But if life has taught me one lesson, it's that nothing is ever simple. Especially love."

Wendy sat in the rocker, listening to Sandy's retreating footsteps. As the quiet night settled around her again, she wondered what force in the universe had made the curious decision that human lives couldn't be simple. It seemed like a dirty trick.

Chapter Seven

Shane was giving Wendy time. Having made his own feelings clear, he had backed away to give her time to think. Or at least that's what she surmised was happening. All she really knew was that she didn't see him again during the following long, hot weeks.

Melange took most of her energy. A new shipment of rainbow-hued stained glass ornaments arrived, and she carefully hung them in all the windows with southern exposures. A zoo of tiny pewter animals arrived, and she spent the better part of one morning arranging them against a blue velvet drape in one of the showcases. Scented candles of every size and color arrived, and she hung them in bunches tied with plaid taffeta ribbons. She kept her fingers busy, but her mind raced full speed ahead on the question of her future or lack of it with one Hall County farmer.

When Shane's patience had been depleted and he came for her, she was no more sure of what to tell him than she had been on the Fourth of July.

Waking up that morning, she had sensed that the day would be eventful. Perhaps it was because the sky was overcast, and the last time Shane had come to Melange it had rained. She showered and dressed with extra care, blowing her hair dry to soften the tight curls that always resulted from extra humidity.

The morning was a business disaster. Thunderstorms dumped sheets of cold, gray rain on the few unsuspecting shoppers who were optimistic enough to come out that morning, and by 11:00 A.M. Melange was empty. Wendy told her assistants to take the day off and wished, for the first time, that she wasn't in charge and could leave, too.

By lunchtime she could no longer ignore the frantic voice inside her that demanded she close and go out for lunch. Even getting soaked was better than sitting in the old Victorian house-turned-gift-shop and listening to the rain scare away her customers. The shop seemed overwhelmingly unreal, no longer an oasis but a prison of pastel colors and delicate ornaments.

She was in the act of pulling on a beige trench coat when Shane arrived. He was wearing the same blue windbreaker and cap beaded with rain, but the expression in his eyes was different. Wendy was reminded, again, that the walls were down between them.

"I've come to take you to lunch."

"Why do you always come in the rain?"

"You've been a farmer's daughter all your life. Surely you should understand."

Wendy noted the weary lines around his eyes. No one knew better than she did just how hard it was to wrest a living from the rich Georgia clay. No matter how much

Shane might want to be with her, he couldn't spare time during good weather. Theirs would have to be a rainy day love affair. No sooner had she thought the words than she wondered about them.

"Let's eat here." She brushed past him to lock the door and turn the sign to Closed. Then she faced him and unbuttoned her coat. "You look too tired to be traipsing around town in the rain looking for a place to eat. I've got the key to Helen's apartment upstairs. We can go up there and I'll fix us sandwiches."

Wendy could tell the domesticity of her suggestion appealed to Shane. Again, she was reminded just how rare had been the times in his life when anyone cared enough about him to fuss over him. She felt a deep tenderness for this man who had once been an unloved little boy. The depth of the feelings he could evoke in her was startling.

"Are you sure?" he asked.

"Absolutely." She led him up the stairs, and he waited while she unlocked the apartment door. She and her assistants often lunched there and the refrigerator was well stocked. Wendy watered Helen's African violets while Shane took off his windbreaker and settled in a comfortable easy chair in the living room. Wendy put water on for coffee and then took out lunch meat and cheese.

Shane's was not an unknown appetite. She had helped feed him often enough during her adolescence, and she had never forgotten his preferences. She remembered that he liked his coffee black and his sandwiches with mustard. She knew he preferred ham to bologna, cheddar cheese to American. She knew that working the soil every day gave him an appetite that would have fattened a white-collar worker like a prime hog before butchering. Accordingly, she piled a fragile bone china plate high with sandwiches to take to the table. She poured them both coffee, diluting her own with milk, and then called him.

There was no answer.

With curiosity she tiptoed into Helen's tiny living room to find him sound asleep.

There was nothing that Shane could have done that would have penetrated right to the core of Wendy's heart more quickly. She was flooded with feelings so powerful that she had no defenses against them. But the absolute fatigue she saw was a warning.

Sinking to a footstool at his feet she watched him as he slept. She had seen her own father this tired. She had seen her oldest brother Greg, who owned a small farm near theirs, this tired. She had seen the look on the faces of men at church who had gotten up before the roosters to finish their chores so that they could enjoy Sunday services. All of them this tired.

And she knew what stood between them and exhaustion so complete that they could not go on.

Their women.

She had watched her mother labor unceasingly, cheerfully, doing chores that city women would never have been able to do, chores that city women didn't even know existed. She had watched the mother she adored, the mother she resembled so strongly, ignoring her own needs time and time again to give to the family and to the land. It wasn't self-sacrifice or martyrdom that made her do it. It was necessity; it was her role in life. It was a role that Wendy wasn't ready for.

And yet, as she watched Shane sleep, watched the way his chest contracted and expanded with each breath, watched the way his face relaxed and softened, she understood why women like her mother had chosen such a difficult existence. They were loved by strong men, men who could tangle with nature itself and come out the winner. They were part of something vital, something more real than the world that Melange represented. They were part of the land, and the land was in their blood and in their hearts.

It was in Wendy's heart, too. She had never been ashamed of her roots. She was proud of her family and what they stood for, proud to be the child of a Georgia dirt farmer because she understood that without people like her father and Shane, the world would be a very hungry place.

But she wasn't sure that it was the life for her. Shane needed a helpmate. It was an old-fashioned term, but there wasn't another one that could convey the truth more fully. He needed a helper, a partner, as well as a lover, a friend. She could decorate his existence, yield her warm body to his every night, but she couldn't guarantee that she could be the kind of wife he needed. Not willingly.

"Fairy child?"

She found his eyes and tried to smile. "You've been asleep."

"And you've been thinking."

"Just about how hard you work."

He sat up a little straighter and fingered her curls. "It's been a week I could forget with a little help. Come here."

She stood, and he pulled her onto his lap and settled her against his chest. "Do you know what it means to me to wake up and find you here?"

She thought she probably did, but she didn't tell him that. Instead she chided him. "You haven't been taking care of yourself."

"There hasn't been time. You saw the shape my house was in, Wendy. Well, the farm's just as bad. Fences are down; there are fields that haven't known a plow for years. Even the broiler houses haven't been taken care of.

Equipment in them isn't working properly; they haven't been disinfected correctly since the last batch of chickens came and went. Once it's under control again I can breathe easier, but until then I'm going to be very busy."

"Well, I've got lunch ready for you now." She tried to pull away, but Shane held her tight. The tenderness she had felt was fast changing to something else. She might be moved by the little motherless boy inside Shane, but it was the man, every virile, devastating inch of him, that held the strongest appeal.

"It's not lunch I want." He laughed at her whispered "oh" and then slowly brushed her hair back from her forehead to cover it with tiny kisses, working his way down her nose, around her mouth and finally to her chin. She lay in his arms, breath suspended, as she waited for him to take her mouth with his. He didn't, tilting her chin instead to find the smooth skin of her neck with his lips, ending in the hollow of her throat. "Lunchtime," he said.

"That's a rotten trick, Shane Reynolds." She wove her fingers through his hair and brought his face back up to hers. "My turn." She followed the same path that he had, rejoicing at the indrawn breath and the low moan in his throat. She took her time, experimenting with different amounts of pressure, different angles for each kiss until finally, his control was exhausted and he pulled her mouth to his.

It had started as a gentle game, but it ended with passion leaping between them. There seemed to be no place in their relationship for slow, gentle loving. Their needs were too immediate, the attraction between them too elemental. She couldn't protest the new intimacies of his hands on her body. He touched her where no one else had ever dared, and she only moaned and pressed herself against his palms. And then, at the same moment, they drew apart, eyes hungry and confused and suddenly wary.

"We're playing with fire. Again." Shane's tone was flat, and Wendy knew he was trying to hide his feelings.

She pushed away and stood in front of him on shaking legs. His familiar silver-blue eyes were examining her for the effects of their lovemaking. There was no good reason to pretend she didn't know what he was talking about. "Shane, one thing I decided after our night together was that I would never allow myself to lose control like that again. I won't change that decision. Not even for you."

"I'm not asking you to change it. I'm not trying to push you into something you're not ready for, but nothing I can do will change what happens when we touch each other."

"Then maybe we shouldn't touch each other."

Shane's grin was crooked and just a bit cocky. "It seems to me that you're the one who just couldn't content herself with a few casual kisses."

Wendy drew in her breath to tell him what she thought of his conceit and then realized that he was teasing her. She choked on a laugh, and in a moment Shane had picked her up to swing her around the living room. He set her down finally, an arm's length from his own body. "Are you going to feed me, woman?"

"The coffee's probably cold, but you can start on the sandwiches while I heat it up." He followed her into the kitchen and she waited on him, enjoying the traditional female role that had never had much appeal for her before.

"How many men have asked you to marry them?" Shane was finishing his second sandwich, reaching for his third.

She was pleased that he thought she was so attractive that men had proposed by the droves. She smiled and lowered her lashes in a direct attempt to be coy. "I couldn't count that high," she said in a breathy, Southern drawl.

"More than ten, less than twenty?"

She stopped pretending. "Actually, only one. I made it very clear to the others that I wasn't interested in anything serious."

"What about the one?"

"He went away after he proposed, and I didn't see him again for seven years."

"And then he came back and proposed again."

Wendy put her sandwich down and wiped her mouth. "Yes," she said softly. "I believe he did."

"And would you happen to know what your answer might be?"

There it was again, the overwhelming desire to say "yes," to throw herself at him and kiss away the vulnerable expression on his beautiful face. To melt into him like the rain outside was melting into the good Georgia earth. She clasped her hands tightly in front of her and examined her fingers. Her knuckles were white. "I don't have an answer yet. He will have to understand that answers take time."

"He understands."

"Then he's a patient man."

"Not endlessly patient," Shane warned. He stood and looked at his watch. "I've got an appointment at the bank." He reached out and ruffled her curls as if to tell her that he understood and wasn't angry. "Will you have dinner with me Monday night? That's the first break I'll have. I thought we could drive into Atlanta if you're not busy."

The city she loved and the man she loved, too. Her eyes widened as she realized how easily the last thought had crept into her conscious mind. It was time to stop pretending that she didn't know how she felt about Shane. "I'll come," she said softly.

"I'll pick you up about five-thirty."

"I'll be waiting."

Wendy leaned back on the burgundy velour bucket seat and watched Shane concentrate on the road in front of them. Monday had been another rainy day and the interstate was slick, but the rain was no longer falling and visibility was good. Actually, Wendy couldn't have cared less about the weather conditions. She was busy drinking in the sight of Shane in a lightweight blue and white striped suit as she listened to his stories about life on a cotton plantation.

"All those stories and you haven't mentioned the owner's daughter yet." She shifted a little to get a better view of his face. His expression was a mixture of masculine pride and humor.

"What do you want to know?" Without taking his eyes off the road, Shane reached over and cupped his hand around the back of Wendy's neck.

"Not much. Just tell me everything."

"That would take all night." His hand tightened on her neck as she tried to wriggle away. "Fair's fair. You have to tell me about all the men in your life if I divulge my secrets."

"That would take a week."

"Your parents may get upset if I keep you in Atlanta that long." Shane squeezed her neck lightly and then put his hand back on the steering wheel. "The owner's daughter, Nelly—"

"Nelly!" Wendy didn't even try to stifle a hoot of laughter. "Shane, how could you be serious about someone named Nelly? We had an old horse named Nelly."

"Nelly was easy to be serious about. She was tall, dark haired and gorgeous. And she did not, I repeat, she did not giggle about other women's names."

"And how many other women's names did you bandy about?"

"Yours. Right before I came back to Hall County."

Wendy sobered immediately. "Oh."

"I told her I had never forgotten you and that I wanted to try and straighten things out between us. And that was the end of that."

"Did she love you?"

"Nelly loved me in her own way. As long as I had stayed on at the plantation, eventually taking it over as her husband, she would have continued to love me. But if I had tried to move her to Hall County and my farm, her love would have withered away. It was highly conditional."

Shane's words hit just a little too close to home to make Wendy comfortable. Wasn't her own love conditional, too? "Maybe she just needed a different life," she said quietly. "Sometimes love can't overcome everything."

"I wouldn't know. I've seen too little of it to judge."

And he needed to see more. Wendy knew that just as surely as she knew anything. Shane needed love, lots of it, unconditional, unreserved, unqualified love. He needed and deserved someone who could give it to him no matter what the circumstances of the life he offered. He broke into her thoughts. "Don't take everything I say so seriously, Wendy. We're here to have fun tonight."

He pulled off the interstate, covering the route to downtown Atlanta as if it were permanently engraved in his mind. Shane, it turned out, was an old movie buff, especially musicals. Since they had snacked at Wendy's house before leaving for the city, they decided to go to the

Fox Theatre on Peachtree Street before dinner to see *South Pacific*.

The Fox building was originally designed as a Moorish courtyard and now ranked as one of the last great movie houses in the United States, second in size to Radio City Music Hall in New York. For a small admission fee, Wendy and Shane heard a recital on the Mighty Moller theater organ, participated in a sing-along and watched the cartoon and movie amidst twinkling stars and moving clouds.

Afterward they bellowed "Some Enchanted Evening," as they strolled back to Shane's car, arms tightly around each other's waists.

"This is our first date," Wendy said as Shane pulled the car onto Peachtree.

"How can that be true?"

"Didn't you notice how much everybody fussed over you when you came to pick me up? Even Jennifer got in the spirit and offered to loan me her one and only pair of designer jeans."

"Your father got in the spirit, too. He told me endless accounts of fatal car accidents on the interstate and equally gruesome stories about what happens to young men who don't bring his daughters home on time."

"I'm glad he didn't scare you off."

"And I'm glad you didn't wear Jennifer's jeans." Shane ran his fingertips over the shoulders of Wendy's coral silk blouse. "I'm also glad that we can finally enjoy each other's company. This is a side of you I know nothing about."

"I didn't know you liked old movies."

"And I didn't know you liked popcorn. Do you have any room left for dinner?"

Wendy tilted her nose to the roof of the car. "I'll have you know that popcorn is mostly air."

"Good, because you'll like the food at Dailey's."

She did. She liked the warehouse setting, renovated to be reminiscent of the twenties. She liked their waiter's flawless recitation of the lengthy dinner menu and the fried yeast rolls that tasted like rich, unsweetened doughnuts. She liked the salad and the plum duckling, and she loved the dessert bar that beckoned from the opposite side of the room as they ate their meal.

"Your eyes are sparkling." Shane covered Wendy's hand with his, and then brought it up to his mouth to kiss. "I've never seen you this relaxed and happy."

"I feel like a different person when I'm away from home." Wendy stroked his cheek enjoying the slight roughness. "And I feel like a different person with you, alone like this, without a squadron of siblings around."

"Country girl, city heart."

"I've never lived in the city so I don't know how much I'd actually like it." She tried to qualify her words so that they wouldn't sound so final. "Maybe I would find that it's not what I imagine, after all."

"I'm afraid you'd like it very much. Atlanta has everything. I've spent a lot of time here myself, and I never found the city boring for even a moment."

It had never occurred to Wendy that Shane might like the city, too. "Could you be happy here?" She found his eyes and held them, and suddenly, she knew just how important his answer would be.

"No." Shane had understood the question, too. But there was no room for compromise in his answer. "If I could do it for you, Wendy, I would, I swear it. But I am what I am, a farmer. Nothing more. I've been offered jobs here, and with my background and skills I could make a good life for us. But I'd hate it, and that would eat away at our relationship."

"Can you understand that the same thing might happen in reverse?"

"I can understand it. But there's one difference. I'm absolutely sure how I feel. You're not."

Wendy's eyes flickered back to her plate and she picked up her fork. "And you hope that my ambivalence is a good sign."

"Yes."

"I don't think I like being seen as wishy-washy."

"Do you want to know how I see you?"

She wasn't sure she did. They were sitting in a dimly lit restaurant on what was actually their first official date, and they should have been exchanging pleasant, romantic conversation. Instead, as always, they were bypassing the niceties and getting right down to the basics. Again she was struck with the unfairness of the way their relationship had been forced to develop.

When she didn't answer, Shane went on anyway.

"I think you're ambivalent because you've never been able to make informed choices. You've always been told what you're supposed to feel and to think. Underneath that lovely, mature exterior is a free spirit who rebels against being pigeonholed. That's part of why you fell in love with me. It was forbidden at the time and exciting. Now you want something completely different from what you've always known, and that means city life."

"I love being reduced to the stereotype of a rebellious adolescent by the man who says he loves me!" Too sophisticated to throw something at Shane, Wendy just glared.

"I know all about rebellious adolescents, remember? I was an unqualified success in the role. No, I don't see you that way at all. I see you as the blithe, wide-eyed fairy child who has to spread her wings. I only wish you had done it sooner. Before I came back.''

''And you're so sure I would have come flying home to you!''

''I have to believe it. I've needed you too much to believe otherwise.''

Her anger evaporated, and she put her fork down for the last time. The waiter removed it and directed them to the dessert bar. At their table once more with chocolate mousse cake for Shane and fresh fruit with white chocolate sauce for Wendy, they sat picking at the fabulous confections. Their appetites seemed to have vanished at the onset of the harsh words.

Finally, Wendy broke the silence. ''Shane, can you wait for me? Can you give me the time I need to spread my wings?''

''You're not just asking for days or even weeks, are you?''

She shook her head.

Shane balled up his napkin and dropped it on the table beside the uneaten cake. ''I've waited seven years. I told you once that I'm not endlessly patient. I need someone to share my life, Wendy.''

She tried to smile. ''At least you didn't say no.''

There was no answering smile. His words were a death knell to her hopes. ''I said no. You just refused to hear it.''

There were no stars, no moon. The trip home had been quiet, both of them busy with their own bleak thoughts. Now they got out of Shane's car and walked in silence up the path to Wendy's front porch.

''First date, last date.'' Shane's voice carried his bitterness.

"Shane, I haven't decided what I should do. You said you wouldn't push me. Give me a little more time." Wendy forced her hands through his arms and clasped them around his waist. His body was all resistance and tension.

"I'm withdrawing my offer."

She didn't even know she was crying until she felt how wet his shirt was under her cheek. His hand brushed her hair with obvious reluctance, finally settling on the back of her head.

"I love you." Wendy's voice was choked with the tears that kept falling.

"I know. It doesn't seem to matter, though. We can't work this out, can we?" He pulled her closer until they were touching everywhere.

"Wait for me. I'll come back home to visit when I can. You can come to Atlanta to see me. We can manage. Give me a year, Shane."

"I can't do it." His hands began to explore her back, moving down below her waist to cup her bottom and bring her even closer. "It wouldn't be fair to either of us. You need freedom, not a cage with an open door. What would you know about yourself at the end of a year if you kept flying back to me?"

"Don't give up on us, Shane."

"I'm not going to make promises I can't keep."

And then the words ended. They held tightly to each other as if they could best the unseen forces that were steadily pulling them apart again. Wendy traced the muscles under the thin cotton of Shane's shirt, kneading them with her fingertips. She resented the intrusion of clothing, wanted the feel of his skin heating beneath her touch. She cried out when his teeth nipped at her lower lip, and she opened for him and for the kiss that seemed to last forever. She knew again the feeling of his body wholly against hers but this time only to tantalize her. She wanted to be closer, to be one with him, never to be separate again.

In that moment, she would have given herself to him once more, if she could have. She would have gladly given everything, her body, her heart, her spirit, her dreams. If she was not to have everything she wanted from life, she would take this part alone and learn to be satisfied. But just as she was drowning, Shane pulled back and thrust her from him.

"Go inside, Wendy."

"I don't want to leave you."

"Go inside."

"I'll marry you. We'll make it work." She held out her hands, palms up as if to implore him.

He stood perfectly still, his face expressionless in the dim light from the porch lamp. "No."

She covered her mouth with her fist, and she saw his reaction to her pain. He shut his eyes. "Wendy, listen."

She heard only night sounds.

"Do you hear the mockingbird?"

Far away she thought she heard the call of some nocturnal bird.

"You're like the mockingbird."

She could feel the tears run down her cheeks again.

"The mockingbird can imitate dozens of other birds, but it never finds its own call. I would never know if what we had was real or an imitation of what it might have been under different circumstances. Fly away, mockingbird. Learn your own song and be happy." He opened his eyes and for a moment, he raised a hand as if to trace the path of her tears. Inches from her face he changed his mind, turning instead to disappear into the shadows.

Somewhere in the distance the mockingbird changed its call, and Wendy knew that it cried for her.

Chapter Eight

Welcome to Virginia-Highland. The Best Living In-
town. City of Atlanta.

Wendy walked past the wooden sign on the narrow strip
of ground bordering two busy streets. She ignored it, just
as she ignored the other landmarks of the community she
now called hers. She had lived in the attractive little
neighborhood long enough to regard it with the jaded eye
of a resident. Atlanta was home and she was no longer a
big-eyed tourist.

Her fingers, encased in thin brown leather, couldn't
seem to grasp the keys to her apartment. The wind whistled shrilly down Virginia Avenue and hit her with an icy
blast that cut right through the puffy stadium coat that had
looked so warm when it had been on the rack at Davison's
department store.

With gratitude she ducked into the entryway of the
small, blond brick apartment building surrounded by
glossy-leafed holly bushes. Out of the wind she peeled off

her gloves and flexed her fingers to restore circulation. This time when she fumbled for her key, she found it. In a moment she was climbing the stairs to her apartment.

Wasn't she supposed to experience a surge of warmth, when, after a long, hard day at work, she came home to her own apartment and realized that the evening was hers? Wendy shook her head at her unrealistic fantasies and busied herself turning on the lights and turning up the thermostat. During the day she kept the apartment just warm enough so that her collection of bromeliads wouldn't freeze. Not that she really cared if they did.

"Bromeliads are the rage now, honey," the friendly woman at the plant store had told her the day she had gone in to buy something living to share her apartment. "You just plunk a little water in here," she said, pointing to a yawning chasm in the middle of the plant, "and you never have to do another thing."

Wendy resented never having to do another thing. She wanted the feel of soil under her fingertips. She, the very same person who had routinely paid her entire allowance to Sandy to weed her share of the vegetable garden, missed digging in the dirt. Her bromeliads didn't even grow in dirt. They grew in sphagnum moss, and some of them hung on boards on the wall.

But she was too poor to start over. One bromeliad and she had developed a reputation as a bromeliad collector. The new friends she had made were always giving her off-shoots of theirs. She sometimes wondered if she would have to rent a larger apartment just to give the exotic plants more space.

On the plus side they did give the apartment color. And it desperately needed color. It was a small apartment, with institutional white walls and practical gray tile floors that covered up the original hardwood. It had come into her possession with a studio couch that doubled as a bed and a round green table with two chairs, one of which had only three legs. So far she had not been able to do more than make bright curtains for the windows and buy one small imitation oriental rug to help cover the blasphemous tile.

Atlanta was expensive, and Wendy had chosen to live in one of its nicer sections, sacrificing a larger, cheaper apartment for safety and pleasant surroundings. Eventually she would paint the walls and buy new furniture. Her landlady had even agreed to have the tile taken up and the floors refinished the next summer. But the apartment had one redeeming feature that made it livable without the changes. It had a tiny screened-in porch facing Virginia Avenue. Although Wendy hated to admit to such an irrational impulse, she knew that she had rented it for that reason alone.

The porch might not be an asset in the cold month of December, but it had helped get her through the loneliest autumn of her life and it would be a godsend when spring arrived.

Wendy stripped off her bright gold skirt and blouse and changed into baggy khaki pants and a tightly ribbed orange sweater. She left on the big, colorful earrings that she always wore now. On the advice of a friend she had gone to a local hair salon and paid a fortune to have her hair cut and styled. Her fluffy curls were gone; her hair was too short to curl except on top where it rebelled in untamed layers. She could have gotten the same cut at her father's barber shop. Now she wore more makeup and more jewelry to emphasize that she was still a very feminine woman.

The new look wasn't altogether unsatisfying. No one would guess that she had just come off a Georgia farm. The image was one of sophistication and style. If she was the same person underneath, it didn't show to the rest of the world. Wendy, herself, could almost forget.

"Wendy!"

"I'm coming." Not bothering with shoes she opened the door to her landlady, Darcy Coleman. Darcy owned the apartment building, a parting gift from her third husband who had given it to her free and clear on the condition that Darcy never get in touch with him again. Darcy said it was the best bargain she had ever made.

"How about dinner tonight?"

Wendy looked at her watch. It was dinnertime, but her stomach had not computed the fact. "I'm not very hungry, and Jason is picking me up at nine to go to The Limelight."

"We can go to Taco Max and have Buffalo wings."

Wendy motioned her friend inside. Darcy was twenty years older than Wendy and experienced to a degree that Wendy found awesome. Darcy had done everything, and now she had settled down in her comfortable apartment to write a book about it. If the book was as interesting as Darcy herself, it would be a best-seller.

Actually, Darcy was another reason why Wendy had settled on this particular apartment. Strangely enough, her parents had approved of Darcy as a fitting chaperon for their daughter. They were not pleased that Wendy had insisted on living alone. In fact there had been a scene that Wendy would never forget. But when her mother had come down to inspect the apartment and meet Darcy, she had given her blessing to the arrangement. Wendy would never know what had passed between the two women. She only knew that Darcy was now her faithful companion.

"I can handle Buffalo wings," Wendy said. "Let me put some shoes on." Darcy flopped on the sofa and watched Wendy lace up ankle high suede boots.

"How was work?"

"I was at the store at Peachtree Center all day. They had a big snafu with a shipment, and I spent the day trying to straighten it out."

"Troubleshooter extraordinaire." Darcy dug her fingers through her long salt-and-pepper hair. "Doesn't that get boring?"

"Uh-huh." Wendy sat up again. "I miss not getting to know customers. I always enjoyed meeting people. Now I'm stuck in the back most of the time with paperwork."

"Assistant anything usually means you get to do everyone's dirty work."

Wendy went into the bathroom to freshen her makeup. "I shouldn't complain. I was lucky to get the job. If my brother-in-law, Tyler Hamilton, hadn't introduced me to Mrs. Britt, I'd be stuck in a five-and-dime somewhere."

"Don't kid yourself. The people who own Atlanta Card and Gift Stores are the lucky ones." Darcy leaned back and closed her eyes. From experience she knew that Wendy wouldn't be out for a few minutes.

"I hope you're right. I found out today that Mrs. Britt is going to retire in February. She's going to recommend that they give me her job."

Darcy whistled. "Six months on the job and you become manager. That would be terrific."

"I'd get a big raise. I'd also go to all the shows to buy for the three shops. It would be great."

"I'll keep my fingers crossed." Darcy looked around the little room with distaste. "Listen, Wendy, the guy in apartment six wants to get rid of a big old reclining chair. Would you like to have it? It's not great but it would perk up this room."

"I'm saving for furniture, but it would help in the meantime." Wendy came out of the bathroom. "Ready?"

"I'm always ready to eat."

Taco Max was less than a block away. In addition to good and plentiful Mexican food the little café served chicken wings, cut and cooked in the Buffalo, New York style and covered with a spicy sauce. Wendy had become addicted.

"What's this infatuation with Jason?" Darcy was starting on her fifth wing.

Wendy cupped her hands behind her ear and lifted her eyebrows. "I think I hear my mother's voice."

"No one has ever accused me of being maternal before."

Wendy examined her friend. At forty-three, Darcy was anything but maternal. If Wendy managed to give the appearance of sophistication, Darcy looked as though she had just stepped out of the jet set. And it was unconscious. Darcy couldn't care less what anyone thought of her. She sensed what the style would be months before the designers came up with it, and she managed to look fabulously wealthy when she was only wearing the jogging suit she wrote in.

"I am not infatuated with Jason. He's a nice man."

"He's a Yuppie."

"Well, he's a nice Yuppie." Wendy had met Jason at a health club near one of the shops where she was assistant manager. The club was in an exclusive hotel, and for a monthly membership fee, Wendy could use the exercise room, sauna and pool. It was one of the incongruities of city life that she had to pay to get the exercise that had been a part of daily living on her parents' farm.

"He's a wimp." Darcy crunched the celery that helped cool off the spiciness of the chicken wings.

"Jason can swim rings around me, and he lifts weights that hurt my back just to look at." Wendy's tone wasn't defensive. She and Darcy always argued about her boy-friends.

"Any man who spends his free time reading books on wine selection and dreaming about his next holiday club vacation is a wimp!" Darcy crunched again to make her point.

Wendy thought about Darcy's words at nine o'clock when Jason came to pick her up. The man looked like anything but a wimp. He was huge, much taller than Shane, the man she used as a yardstick for everyone else. His shoulders were broad, his waist and hips narrow. He dressed in expensive, conservative suits that fit his stock-broker image and coordinated with his blond hair and blue eyes. Wendy knew that female hearts all over Atlanta melted when Jason Billings walked by.

And he danced like a dream. The Limelight, one of Atlanta's premier nightspots, was the perfect place for Jason to strut his stuff. Complete with mimes, artificial snow and a stainless steel dance floor, The Limelight appealed to Jason's sense of the trendy. Wendy enjoyed it as an experience from another world. She enjoyed Jason for the same reason.

It was well past 2:00 A.M. when he brought her home.

"When are you going to let me stay for the night?"

Wendy wondered if Darcy would consider this big, hulking specimen of masculinity a wimp, now. Jason was almost panting with lust.

"Look, Jason. I've told you before, if that's what you want from a relationship you're spending your money on the wrong woman."

"I can make you change your mind." His arms closed around her and he squeezed lightly. "You're a big girl now, Wendy."

"An old-fashioned, big girl." She dug her elbows under his ribs. "I'm not going to bed with you."

"Then who do you go to bed with?"

Wendy shook her head. She knew the question was asked out of genuine curiosity. Jason couldn't conceive of anyone who didn't sleep around. "Nobody, Jason. I sleep alone."

"That's a real waste."

"My body isn't a commodity you have to worry about." She wrenched out of his arms and turned to unlock her apartment door. "If you can't understand, then don't bother to come back."

"Do you want to get married?" Jason's forehead was wrinkled at the complexity of the situation.

Wendy's laughter tinkled in the empty hall. "If that's a proposal, it's the strangest one I've ever heard."

"Lord, I wasn't proposing. I was just trying to figure out if—" He stopped short.

"If I like men?" Wendy laughed again. "I assure you I do. Just not in my bed unless I have a ring on the fourth finger of my left hand. Sorry, Jason, you snagged a dinosaur this time."

Wendy closed the door behind her, aware that Jason was still standing in the hallway trying to figure out how to get around her moral code. She cleansed all the makeup from her face and brushed her teeth. The slinky black dress she had worn landed in a heap at the foot of the couch, and she pulled on an old football shirt that had belonged to one of her brothers. Somehow, with each movement, the humor of the scene with Jason disappeared.

She lay in the darkness wondering how many times she would live out that particular confrontation again. She was a city girl with country values. Obviously not all city girls slept around and not all country girls were chaste, but now the people Wendy associated with took casual intimacy for granted. The people who had raised her did not.

And then, as always, right before she fell asleep she thought of Shane. There had never been anything casual about their intimacy. She loved him now as much or more than she ever had. Her body ached for his, her heart cried out to him. But every day she moved farther and farther away from his arms. She no longer knew if there was a way back.

She had been home once in the five months since moving to Atlanta. She had not seen Shane at all. Finally, she had gotten up the nerve to ask Sarah what she knew about him.

Shane, she was told, was seriously dating another woman, Nancy Gwynn, a farmer's widow with a small son. Everyone expected Nancy and Shane to marry. Wendy, like the mockingbird, was searching for her own call. Shane, it seemed, had found his.

It was while she was waiting in line to mail her Christmas packages home that Wendy decided to go back to Hall County for the holiday. All the Atlanta Card and Gift Stores stayed open until nine o'clock Christmas Eve, but then they closed until the day after New Year's. It was an expensive tradition, but one that the owners adhered to every year.

For most of December, Wendy had told herself that she needed to spend the Christmas vacation painting her apartment and searching for reasonably priced furniture. It was a thinly veiled excuse not to have to face Shane or the gossip about him. She wasn't sure she could handle either.

But as she stood in line, waiting to send the presents that she had carefully shopped for, she realized what a coward she was becoming. She missed her family. She wanted them around her at this, her favorite time of the year. She needed to go back to her roots, if only for a few days.

Christmas Eve at 9:05 P.M. she pulled her car into the Atlanta traffic and headed for the interstate.

They were all waiting up for her. Even her father who would have to rise before dawn on Christmas day was awake. Wendy was passed from family member to family member, kissed, exclaimed over and hugged to death. With the exception of two of her older brothers and Stacey's family, everyone was home for the holiday. Stacey had sent her regrets with the pictures of her new baby son, six-week-old Jeremy Ryan. By the time Wendy got to see the pictures, they were tattered and dog-eared and much loved.

Wendy fell asleep in her own bed with the sound of Sandy's, and Sarah's and baby Bonnie's even breathing breaking the country stillness. She was very glad to be home.

"I'm having trouble getting used to the new you." Sandy patted Wendy's head as if her sister were a prize French poodle. Wendy was down on her hands and knees following Bonnie who was holding on to the edge of a giraffe on wheels as she toddled around the room.

"What do you think of the new me?" Wendy grabbed the giraffe and turned it so that Bonnie was heading back into the middle of the room.

"I think it's the same old you dressed in city wrappings."

"I think so, too."

Sandy flopped down on the floor beside her sister and pushed her long, golden braid over her shoulder. "I'm glad you decided to come home. Ma was pretty upset when you said you weren't."

"This morning was wonderful." It had been a traditional MacDonald Christmas. Now the rest of the family had gone out to visit nearby relatives while Sandy and Wendy opted to stay at home with Bonnie. After the noise and confusion of the holiday, the peaceful house was a welcome relief.

Sandy squeezed Wendy's knee. "How is your life, really?"

Wendy tried to answer honestly. "Lonely sometimes, exciting sometimes. You should know, you lived in Cameron by yourself for a while before you married Tyler."

"But I wasn't in love with a man I left behind."

Wendy didn't answer.

"Shall I drop it?"

Wendy shook her head. "I didn't want to leave Shane behind. But he didn't love me enough to give me the time I needed. He made demands. I couldn't give in. Now I understand he's going to marry Nancy Gwynn."

"I remember her." Sandy held out a plastic cup to Bonnie who sat down with a plop and then crawled over to sit on her mother's lap. "She was Nancy Burns when she was in Stacey's and Shane's class in high school. Her husband Robert was killed a couple of years ago in an accident."

"Sarah says she has a son. He'll give Shane a head start on the family he wants so badly." Nothing Wendy could do would hide the bitterness in her voice.

"And just like that you're going to let Nancy Burns Gwynn have the man you've loved since you were a kid."

"Leave it alone, Sandy!"

The room was quiet except for the sound of Bonnie blowing bubbles in her cup.

Finally Wendy broke the silence. "I'm sorry."

"You always were sorry when you yelled at me."

"I probably yelled at you twice in all our years together." Wendy smiled a misty smile. "Do you really think I'm making a mistake?"

"The whopper of your life."

"If Shane loved me, would he be this close to marrying another woman?"

"And how do you know just how serious their relationship is? Sarah can only report what she sees and hears, not what Shane is feeling. Only Shane can tell you that."

"But Shane's not here to tell me anything."

Sandy stood, hauling Bonnie with her. "Then you'll have to go to him."

"I bought him a Christmas present. Do you believe it?"

"Yes."

"I'm scared."

"Good. You should be." Sandy examined her sister. "I realize it's ridiculous for me to advise you about fashion, but wear something soft and feminine when you see him. I'm not sure Shane will understand your hair or those clothes."

Wendy looked down at her white jeans splattered with fluorescent designs and the fluorescent orange sweater that stylishly persisted in slipping over one shoulder to reveal a white undershirt. "I think I'll have to borrow something of yours."

"That will be a first."

It wasn't until Christmas dinner was a fond memory that Wendy felt she could slip away. She borrowed a green cashmere sweater and dark plaid skirt from Sandy and took extra time to be sure her makeup was subtle and flattering. There was nothing she could do about her hair except hope that it grew quickly. To compensate she wore her best gold earrings.

She had not intended to buy Shane a gift, but then she had found the original cast album of *South Pacific* in a junk shop near her apartment. The record was in perfect condition, and she knew he would enjoy it. She also knew that every time he played it, he would be reminded of her. It was too perfect to resist.

Sandy suggested that she telephone Shane, but Wendy's courage failed at the thought. She knew that if she talked to him she would not have the nerve to ask if she could come to his house to deliver his Christmas gift. She decided to make it look as though she were traversing the neighborhood, dropping off presents to all her friends. It was a scheme as full of holes as a pound of Swiss cheese, but it was the best idea she could come up with.

Although it wasn't late, the sky was winter-dark when she left her parents' farm to drive to Shane's house. She took the long way, just as she had the last time she had gone to him, and she was surprised at how fast her car went even though her foot barely touched the accelerator. She was on the road that bordered Reynolds' property much sooner than she wanted to be.

In the cold, still winter night Shane's house looked warm and inviting. The front porch light was on as if he had expected her to come. She saw immediately that both his car and truck were parked in front. Shane was home.

Shane was home, and she was parked outside of his house trying to get up the nerve to step out of the car and up to his front porch. Shane was home and she was sitting, like a fool, glued to the vinyl seat of her car.

"Come on, Wendy. Get your act together. You can do it." Resolutely she swung her legs to the ground and started up the walk.

Shane had obviously heard her drive up because the front door opened, and he came out onto the porch. He was wearing dark slacks and a dress shirt covered with a pale blue sweater. He stood with his hands thrust into his pockets as she approached.

Wendy had forgotten just how much she loved to look at him. She had forgotten how striking his copper-tinted skin and his pale eyes were and the way the silkiness of his hair contrasted with his totally masculine features. She had forgotten how taut his body could be when he was waiting for her to hurt him.

"Hello, Shane. Merry Christmas."

"Merry Christmas, Wendy."

She climbed the steps, wondering how there could be so many when the porch was only four feet off the ground. "I brought you a Christmas present."

"Did you?"

He wasn't hostile, but he seemed totally unapproachable. Wendy tried to think of something to break the impasse between them. "I've missed you."

The only sign he gave that he'd heard her was a slight lifting of his shoulders as if he had sighed without his own knowledge. Wendy wanted to disappear through the porch. She wanted to lie on the cold, hard ground and throw a tantrum that would last until New Year's Day. Instead she held the present out to him. "I thought of you when I saw this. I couldn't resist."

Shane kept his eyes on her face as he tore the bright green wrapping off the album. Then he smiled. It wasn't the warmest smile she had ever seen, but it was a start. "Do you sing 'I'm Gonna Wash That Man Right Out-a My Hair,' every chance you get?"

"No. I tend toward 'This Nearly Was Mine.'" Wendy stepped a little closer. She gave herself an unconscious hug. She was cold both inside and out. "I really have missed you."

"It's a thoughtful gift. Thank you." His eyes focused on her mouth and for a moment, Wendy held her breath. Then he stepped forward and bent the distance to kiss her cheek. "You're freezing. I'd invite you in, but—"

"Shane?" A soft call from the house alerted Wendy to the reason why they were still standing outside. The front door opened, and a pretty young woman with long brown hair stepped onto the porch. "Oh, I'm sorry. I didn't know where you were."

"It's all right, Nancy. Come meet Wendy MacDonald. Wendy, this is Nancy Gwynn." Shane stepped back to give the two women a clearer view of each other. Nancy was taller than Wendy and wholesome with a smile that could sell milk by the gallons. Wendy could imagine Nancy planning the day's menus as she fed chickens with one hand and hoed the corn with the other. It was not a pleasant thought.

"Shane's told me about the MacDonald family. I knew Stacey well. So you're her baby sister."

The amazing thing was that there seemed to be absolutely no malice in Nancy's remark. She sounded as wholesome as she looked.

"I'm happy to meet you, Nancy." Wendy forced herself to smile. "I've got other presents to deliver so I'd better be off."

"Please don't go. Come inside and warm up first. It's freezing out here. I'll make you some coffee." Once again Nancy sounded completely sincere.

Wendy couldn't imagine anything worse in the world than watching another woman bustle around Shane's kitchen. "No thank you. I really do have to go." She turned to find her way down the porch steps.

"Mommy. Where's Shane?" A little boy dressed in fuzzy yellow pajamas stood in the doorway holding a worn white blanket. "There him is!" With a whoop the little boy hurled himself into Shane's waiting arms.

"There *he* is, partner." Shane turned back to Wendy. "This is Robby Gwynn the third. Robby, this is Wendy."

Robby squinted at Wendy. He obviously didn't like what he saw, and he rested his head on Shane's shoulder to avoid looking at her anymore.

Wendy took a deep breath and allowed the cold air to bite at her lungs. "He's quite a young man, Nancy."

"He keeps me busy."

"I want my pie now," Robby said with a pout.

Nancy gave an embarrassed shrug. "We were just finishing dinner."

"I'm sorry if I disturbed you. You all get back inside." Wendy found her way down the steps and out to the sidewalk. She made herself turn and wave before she got to the car. "Merry Christmas."

Nancy had gone back into the house, but Shane stood on the porch with Robby in his arms. He was still there when Wendy turned the car around and drove away.

Chapter Nine

Through her apartment window, Wendy could see the buds on the dogwood trees across the street. Spring had arrived in Atlanta, but she couldn't have cared less.

"So, what did the Georgia peach think of the Big Apple?" Darcy perched on the edge of Wendy's new sofa as she watched her friend unpack.

Wendy lifted her shoulders in an indifferent shrug. "It's a wonderful city. I was too busy to see much of it, but what I saw I liked. Even in March."

"Did you come back with lots of new stuff for your shops?"

"Lots. Next time though I think I'll order through catalogues." Wendy sat down. "I had imagined that seeing some of the world would be the best part of my new job as manager, but I don't think traveling agrees with me."

Darcy looked at her watch and stood. "Well, it agrees with me, and I'm off to do some."

"Where are you going?"

"I'm going to the races." Darcy smiled at Wendy's puzzled expression. "Remember Donnie-boy, my second husband, the jockey?"

"I thought Donnie-boy was the horse he rode."

"Donnie's invited me to come stay in Louisville with him for a week. I thought it might be fun."

"Have a good time." Wendy leaned her head against the back of the sofa and shut her eyes.

"Wendy, are you all right?"

"I think I'm coming down with a cold or something. I just need a good night's sleep to ward it off."

Darcy put her hand on Wendy's forehead and shook her head. "You're hot. You'd better get in bed right now."

Obediently, Wendy stood and pulled the cushions off the sofa. In a moment it was a comfortable double bed already made up with pretty flowered sheets. Wendy flopped down, still fully clothed.

"Wendy, I hate to leave you like this, but if I don't go right now, I'll miss my plane. Is there someone you can call if you need help?" Darcy felt Wendy's forehead again and wrinkled her nose.

"Sure. Go on. Have a good time."

"Let me get you some aspirin and juice first."

"I don't think I have either."

"I'll bring you what I have on my way out. Promise me you'll call somebody if you need help."

"I'll be fine, Darcy. It's just a cold." It seemed an appropriate diagnosis for what was wrong with her. Wendy had never felt so cold in her entire life.

An hour later she was burning up. She had just enough strength to open the door to her little screened-in porch to let the brisk spring breeze cool her apartment. Twenty minutes later she was cold again, but this time she didn't have the energy to get up and close the door.

She dozed fitfully. Sometimes she was confused when she awoke to find herself in the strange apartment. Home was a pink bedroom in an old Georgia farmhouse. Home was the sound of cows and birds and children laughing. Once she woke up from a dream where Shane's arms were around her holding her. He was so warm, so warm. . . .

The shrill ringing of the telephone brought her temporarily back into consciousness. She tried to ignore its insistent summons, but it was stronger than she was. The caller was Jason.

"I thought you might like to go dancing with me tonight."

"I'm sick, Jason. I won't be going anywhere for a while."

Jason, the health club maniac, reeled off a long list of vitamins and special food supplements she should start taking immediately.

"I don't happen to keep a chemistry lab in my kitchen," Wendy said shortly.

It seemed that was too bad. She should have been prepared. Jason was sorry, but he was afraid that he might catch the flu if he came over himself. Instead he dictated the number of a pharmacy that delivered. Wendy told him sweetly what he could do with his phone number.

The phone rang again, only this time it seemed to be dark outside. That was hard to understand since it had been light just a few moments before when she had talked to Jason.

"Wendy?" It was her mother.

"Hi." Wendy tried desperately to put some pep in her voice. "How are you?" Long distance phone calls were rare. Wendy wished she felt good enough to appreciate the special treat.

"How are *you*? Darcy called us from Kentucky to say you were sick. She worried about you during her whole trip."

"I'm doing fine. I just need to rest."

"What's your temperature?"

Wendy hesitated just long enough to give herself away.

"You don't have a thermometer, do you?"

"No, but I have a phone number." Wendy began to giggle, but the exertion sent shooting pains through her head.

"A phone number? Honey, what are you talking about?"

"I have a phone number of a thermometer." Wendy giggled again, and this time tears sprang to her eyes in response. "I have to go, Ma. I'll call you back tomorrow when I'm feeling better." She hung up, taking the phone off the hook. She fell asleep listening to the steady beep that was the phone company's warning that no one could get in touch with her now.

"Wendy!" The beeping telephone had changed to a loud banging on the door. "Wendy, can you hear me?"

Wendy had been dreaming of Shane again. Now she heard his voice calling through the thick, black fog that enveloped her. She fought her way through it, determined to find him.

"Wendy!"

She sat up slowly and opened her eyes. The thick, black fog was a reality. The door to the porch was wide open, and cold damp night air blanketed the small room. Her covers were soaked and so were the heavy sweater and wool pants that had been appropriate for March in New York. "Shane?"

"Open the door, sweetheart. Can you do that?"

Her body felt like the fog, loose and liquid and elusive. She floated slowly across the room, and turned the key that unlocked the door. If she was dreaming, she didn't want to wake up.

"Good God, Wendy. You're burning up."

She felt Shane's arms around her and she leaned gratefully against him. She was even more grateful when she felt him lift her high and carry her back across the room.

"Are you real?" she asked.

"Completely real."

"Was it real earlier when you were holding me and kissing me?" She dropped her head against his shoulder, too tired to hold it up anymore.

He didn't answer, setting her carefully on the bed, before he closed the door to the porch.

"Was it real?"

"No."

A tear ran down her cheek, followed closely by another. "It felt real."

"I wanted to be holding you and kissing you. You picked up my fantasies." Shane sat on the bed beside her, smoothing back the hair that curled in a damp riot around her face.

"Don't go away, Shane. You keep going away."

"I'm not going anywhere. Right now we're going to get your fever down. When was the last time you took any aspirin?"

Wendy closed her eyes. "Darcy gave me some before she left a little while ago."

"That's been hours, sweetheart. Have you had anything to drink since she left?"

"Shane, you'll catch the flu."

"It'll be worth it."

"Then I can take care of you, if Nancy will let me." She opened her eyes. "I'd forgotten about Nancy. Are you married?"

"No. Wendy, don't worry about anything right now." He went into the kitchen and found the apple juice and aspirin that Darcy had left on the counter. He set them on the small table that matched Wendy's new sofa. "I'm going to lift you up and take off your sweater and pants unless you think you can do it by yourself. We've got to get you cooled down."

She shook her head. "I'm too weak."

Immediately he moved her to a sitting position. "Lift your arms."

Obediently she lifted her hands high above her body and felt the heavy wool slide over her head. The pants were next and she was left in a nylon teddy, too exhausted to think of modesty. Shane propped pillows behind her and disappeared into the bathroom. The light filtering through the doorway hurt Wendy's eyes. In a minute he reappeared with a cold washcloth.

"I want you to take the aspirin and finish this juice. Then I'm going to give you a sponge bath."

"My parents would disown us both if they knew what you were doing to me." She held the glass with a trembling hand and swallowed the pills he gave her. Then she lay back against the pillows again.

"Your parents know I'm here." Shane smoothed the wet cloth over her forehead and her cheeks, repeating the path in a slow circular motion. "Does that feel good?"

"Mmm... What do you mean my parents know you're here?"

"I was at your house when Darcy called. After your mother talked to you she was frantic. She's thrown her back out again so she couldn't come herself. Jennifer's got her driver's license now, but your parents wouldn't let her drive to Atlanta alone. So I convinced them I was the only one who could make the trip.'' Shane left to wet the washcloth again. When he returned he began to smooth it over Wendy's neck.

"What about your farm?"

"I've got two hired men who can keep things under control until I get back."

"What about Nancy?"

"Don't worry about Nancy."

Wendy put her hand over the washcloth that was moving in slow circles over the portion of her chest that was exposed. "What about Nancy?"

"Until I'm married, I don't have to answer to anyone."

Too weak to argue, Wendy dropped her hand and shut her eyes. She drifted off to sleep while Shane did things with the washcloth that would have heated her blood to boiling point if she hadn't been so sick.

"Wendy. Wake up. It's time for more aspirin. You're burning up again."

"I'm so cold." This time she couldn't sit up, and Shane threaded his arm behind her back and lifted her like a rag doll.

"Jason lifts weights and I bet he couldn't lift me that easily." Wendy shivered.

"Here, drink this." Shane held the glass for her this time as she swallowed the aspirin. "Who's Jason?"

"Jason's a wimp who keeps trying to get into this bed with me."

"I don't think you're going to enjoy remembering you told me that when you wake up tomorrow." Shane set the glass down and tucked her back in.

"I keep telling him 'no.' There's only one man I want in my bed."

"Go to sleep, Wendy."

"Sleep with me, Shane. I'm so cold. Warm me up."

"Go to sleep, sweetheart."

"I'll bet you sleep with *her*." She waited. "Don't you?"

"Someday I'll remind you of this conversation."

"Go home, Shane. Go home to Nancy." With great effort Wendy turned on her side and buried her face in the pillow. She shivered again as she waited for the door to slam.

Instead she heard the bedsprings creak as Shane sat on the edge. In a moment her feverish brain registered the sounds of his shoes hitting the floor, one by one. Then Shane's arms were around her. She wasn't too sick to realize that he had taken off his shirt and pants. "There's only one woman I want to sleep with," he said softly. "And now I'm doing it."

The sunshine hurt her eyes through her eyelids. Cautiously Wendy lifted her lids, one by one, to see how much more the light would hurt with her eyes open. It wasn't as bad as she thought. She lay still as her vision adjusted. Her head felt heavy, every cell in her body ached and there was a weight pressing her into the mattress. There was also a hand dangling suspiciously close to her breast.

"Good Lord!"

"So you're awake. How do you feel?"

The suspicious hand moved to her hair and stroked it back from her face. The weight, a leg, was suddenly gone and Wendy knew Shane had put distance between them. She discovered immediately that it was only to give her room as he turned her to face him.

"How do you feel?" he repeated.

"Confused." Her voice was a hoarse croak.

"I'll bet." His hand brushed her forehead again and then lingered as he felt for fever. "You're cool. I felt the fever break early this morning. You soaked us both."

His face was haggard but relieved. Wendy lifted her hand to brush his cheeks, which were the texture of the roughest sandpaper. The slight effort took all her strength. "Am I dreaming this?"

"I hope in your dreams you're not in bed with me just because you're sick."

"I'd blush, but it would take too much energy." She couldn't seem to stop exploring Shane's face with her fingers. She traced the lines around his eyes, lingered on the heavy eyelids, moved in trembling inches across his lower lip. "Why are you here?"

"To get you well."

"I mean, why are you in my bed?"

"Because you invited me."

"I don't remember."

"I'm glad." He laughed as her eyes widened.

"Oh, no!"

"It's all right. People say strange things when they're delirious."

"Discount everything I said, immediately."

"I don't think so. For instance, you told me that you haven't been to bed with Jason the wimp. I wouldn't want to discount that." He laughed again as she bit her lip.

"You're enjoying this, aren't you?"

"Yes. And aren't you enjoying it just a little, too?" His hand smoothed over her shoulder, nudging the lace strap of her teddy as he did.

Wendy was suddenly acutely aware of the intimacy of their positions, the unclothed or nearly unclothed state of each of them, and the fact that Shane was not unaffected by either. Before she could point out the dangers lurking on the horizon, he dropped a kiss on her forehead and turned to sit on the edge of the bed. Wendy was treated to a broad expanse of solid, well-muscled back as he reached down and began to pull on his pants. He faced her as he slipped on his shirt, and she watched his chest disappear as he fastened the buttons.

"Are you leaving?"

"Not until I'm sure you're going to be all right by yourself." Shane ran his fingers through his hair. "Right now I'm going to run a bath for you. Can you manage by yourself if I get you in there?"

She didn't know, but she knew she wasn't going to let him stay in the bathroom with her and find out. "I'll manage."

When he came back she sat up with difficulty, and with Shane's arm around her waist she made it into the bathroom. The bath was warm and just what she needed to soak away the aches and pains that were the aftermath of her fever. She even washed her hair.

"I can't find anything decent for you to wear," Shane called through the bathroom door.

"My clothes are all decent!"

"I mean nightgowns. If you aren't sleeping with Jason the wimp, why do you have such erotic night wear?"

Wendy sank lower into the tub, and she bit her lower lip to keep from laughing. She owned one pair of satin pajamas that had been a Christmas gift from Sandy. Everything else she wore was serviceable cotton. "My robe's in the closet. I promise I'll keep it on the whole time you're here."

"That and lingering germs should keep you pure as the driven snow." The bathroom door opened and Wendy's robe and a pink cotton nightgown landed on the floor. The door slammed shut once more.

It took Wendy twice as long as usual to dry herself off and dress. By the time she finished, she was totally exhausted again. She made it to the bathroom door and smiled weakly. "Can you help me back to bed?"

Shane was at her side in a moment. She noticed that the sheets had been changed. "You look about thirteen with your hair wet and no makeup," he told her.

"I feel like I'm ninety. I don't ever remember being this sick." Wendy settled herself on the freshly made bed and smiled up at Shane. "I can't thank you enough for coming when I needed you."

"That's what friends are for."

"We haven't been friends since I was thirteen."

"Can you eat something for breakfast?"

Obviously discussing their personal situation was off-limits. Wendy was just as glad. She felt too vulnerable to talk about something so important. "I don't have anything in my refrigerator, I'm afraid. I've been in New York for the past week."

"You'll be surprised what I can do with nothing."

Breakfast appeared ten minutes later in the guise of two scrambled eggs, a thick slice of ham, a corn muffin and fresh orange juice.

"How did you manage this?" The man was a magician.

"Your mother sent enough supplies to keep you eating high on the hog for another week." He recited in a singsong voice: "Four quarts of chicken soup, six large cans of orange juice, a small ham, one pineapple upside-down cake, two dozen cornbread muffins, two dozen eggs, a casserole of green beans, six boxes of tissues, one large bottle of aspirin, four different kinds of cold remedies and a heating pad." He shot her a crooked grin. "If you'd known about the heating pad, would you have invited me to sleep with you last night?"

"I still don't think I invited you." Wendy's eyes got suspiciously moist as she thought about the love his list represented. "Isn't my family wonderful? How did my mother manage all this with a bad back?"

"She directed traffic. Jennifer got most of it together."

"It's too bad Sarah's away at school. If she'd been at home she could have saved you the trip." Wendy took a bite of the corn muffin and chewed carefully. She wasn't sure how her body would tolerate food.

"I wanted to come."

Wendy didn't know what to say. She stopped chewing and raised her eyes to his.

"You've got muffin crumbs on your chin." Shane reached over and cupped one hand under her face as his other hand brushed the crumbs away.

"Aren't you going to eat?" She felt suddenly shy.

"I made myself breakfast, too. It's still in the kitchen." He stood up, and in a moment he was back on the bed with an identical plate of food.

They talked casually. Shane wanted to know about Wendy's job, and Wendy wanted to know how Shane's plan to convert some of his acreage to organic truck farming was going.

He finished his breakfast and most of hers as they talked. "So far I haven't grown anything on that land except cover crops to enrich the soil. I've been steadily adding manure and rock fertilizers, cottonseed meal, bone meal from one of the local meat-packing plants. I'll be ready to plant next month."

"Is there such a market for organic produce that it makes all the extra effort worthwhile?" Wendy set her plate down. She couldn't manage another bite.

"There's a good market here in Atlanta. Organic produce, locally grown, will be snapped up. Whether it's worth it financially remains to be seen. Since all the farms around me use chemicals, a lot of the natural means of controlling harmful insects won't be much help."

"Like what?"

"Well, there are good insects and bad insects. Pesticides don't usually discriminate. The insects that don't harm crops but do eat bad insects get killed right along with the bad insects."

"So cultivating certain kinds of insects on your land isn't helpful because other farmers will kill them off." Wendy sympathized with Shane's dilemma.

"It's too bad bugs can't read signs. I could post my land."

Wendy smiled. She might still feel as though she had been stomped by a hundred horses the night before, but it was almost worth it to be sitting on her bed having a conversation with the man she loved. "Could you persuade your neighbors to try organic methods?"

"Would your father risk his livelihood for an ideal he's not even sure is viable?" Shane shook his head. "Actually, the truth is that I've only given five acres to the experiment, myself. I'm one of those people killing off the good bugs, too."

"In other words, it's easy to be moralistic when it's a backyard vegetable patch and not easy when your mortgage is at stake."

"Spoken like a true farmer's daughter."

"Why are you doing it, then?"

"I want to put something back into the land for my children. We continue to deplete the soil day after day, just like we deplete all the world's resources. It seems to me that all of us are responsible for seeing that we don't take more than our share."

"I think you're right. Someday our children will thank you for your farsightedness." She blinked when she realized what she had just said. "I meant, of course, our children in the broader sense—you know, our children, our world . . ."

"I thought maybe you were proposing." Shane picked up her plate and took it back into the kitchen, and Wendy could hear the sounds of dishes being washed.

"Would it do any good if I did?" Wendy couldn't resist. "Aren't you already taken?"

"Close."

She pulled off her robe, slid back down under the covers and turned over on her side. Suddenly she realized just how sick she still felt. She wanted to tell Shane that she would take care of herself and that he was free to go back home to his beloved Nancy, but by the time he emerged from the kitchen she was fast asleep.

It was late afternoon when she woke up again. At first she thought that Shane had left, but then she heard the sound of the shower. She wondered how he had spent the long day. When he came out of the bathroom she was sitting up with the sheet tucked under her arms. If he truly thought an opaque cotton nightgown was erotic, she didn't want to give him any ideas.

"I hope I didn't wake you." Shane stood in the doorway buttoning his shirt with one hand. It was a wonderfully masculine habit, one she had been exposed to at home for years, and for a moment she just watched in fascination.

"No," she said, finally lifting her eyes to his. "I'm feeling much better. I think I've slept off the worst of this."

"Good. How about something to eat?"

"You don't have to wait on me anymore. I appreciate what you've done, but I know you've got commitments back in Hall County."

"If you're really all right, I'll go back after dinner. But not before. Now, how about some chicken soup?"

Wendy shrugged listlessly.

She managed to eat most of a bowl of soup. It was rich with vegetables and egg noodles, just the way she remembered it, and it made her feel worse, not better. She was suddenly terribly homesick. "My mother always makes this soup when somebody's not feeling well. It's a good thing I didn't move to San Francisco. My body wouldn't have known it was supposed to get better without some of Ma's chicken soup."

"If you had moved to San Francisco, your mother still would have found a way to get some to you." Shane set their bowls on the end table. "Ready to get some more sleep?"

Wendy shook her head and put her hand on his arm. "I'm ready to talk."

Shane seemed to understand that she wasn't suggesting trivial conversation. He pulled away so that her hand lay on the bed between them. "Don't say things you'll regret as soon as you're feeling better. You're tired and weak and vulnerable. This is no time to be making decisions."

"And when will we have another chance? It's been eight months since our last conversation, excluding Christmas, and you haven't called me once!" Wendy could feel the tears collecting. He was right. She was in no shape to talk about anything important, but by the time she was, he would be married to Nancy.

"I told you I was setting you free."

"But I don't want *you* to be free!"

"Double standards, Wendy?"

"Shane, are you using Nancy to make me jealous? Because if you are, it's working." A big tear escaped and ran down her cheek.

"You should know I wouldn't use a woman that way."

She recognized the steely glint in his eye, but she pushed on. "Then tell me why you're here! And don't give me any mumbo jumbo about being the only person who could come. One of my little brothers could have driven Jennifer or come by himself. Every one of them knows how to take care of a sick person. It's not much different from doctoring a cow!"

"It's not nearly as pleasant!"

"Tell me!"

"I was frantic with worry, that's why. I couldn't stand the thought of you here ill and alone, and it wasn't good enough for me to have someone else take care of you. I wanted to make sure you were all right myself."

"Oh." Wendy's anger vanished and another tear followed the path of the first one. "Do you still love me, Shane?"

"Don't ask me that." He stood and walked to the glass door looking out over her tiny screened porch.

"I still love you. I always will," she said just loudly enough for Shane to hear.

"Eight months ago we decided that love wasn't enough. I don't think that's changed."

"What you mean is that you haven't changed. You still want it all."

"You want it all, Wendy. You want me to hang on, hoping that you'll get this damned city out of your system, while I stay at home, put in seventeen-hour work days and come home every night to an empty house and a cold kitchen. All on the off chance that you'll realize someday that you can be happy as a farmer's wife."

He turned back to her. "You want me to sacrifice a good relationship with a woman who shares the same values that I do, a woman who wants a home and a family and a husband who puts her first. Are you telling me that I have a reason to stop seeing Nancy? That you want me no matter what the problems? That you're willing to be the wife I need?"

Wendy didn't know what she was telling him. Her head was aching with a fierce pain that was only partly induced by her illness. She put her head in her hands and let her tears wash away some of the tension exploding inside her.

"I'm sorry, sweetheart. God, I'm sorry." Shane came to sit on the bed beside her. He put his arms around her and pulled her close. "You're in no shape for this. I told you this wasn't the right time."

"There's never going to be a right time, is there, Shane?" She was desperate. She could not face another goodbye. Wendy wound her arms around Shane's neck and pressed her body to his. She couldn't seem to get close enough. Frantically she tried, kissing his chin, his ears and finally his mouth when he turned toward her.

She felt the jolt of their reunion in every cell of her body. She could feel her breasts in the thin nightgown as they flattened against his hard chest and the tautness of her nipples as desire flooded through her. Deep inside she knew that she could withhold nothing from him. She was fertile ground that had remained fallow too long.

Shane's hand found her breast, and she could hear the moan low in his throat. Without conscious thought she slipped a strap low over one shoulder and guided his hand inside her gown. This time the moan was her own. Her hands sought closer contact, pulling his shirt from his jeans to stroke the warm, rippling flesh of his back. It wasn't enough. She wanted to feel all of him, and with shaking fingers she tried to unbutton his shirt. He pulled away long enough to do it himself and then, as his eyes locked with hers, he slipped her gown over both shoulders and let it fall to her waist.

Slowly Shane pushed her back against the pillows and covered the top of her body with his. Wendy wrapped her arms around him again, only this time she could feel so much more. Their kiss went on and on until she felt dizzied from it. Dizzied, and aching, and trembling and feverish. None of it had anything to do with her illness. It was all for him.

Shane's hands were becoming reacquainted with her flesh as they memorized each curve. The immature feelings that had flourished for such a short time so many years before were completely eclipsed by this new, darker passion. Wendy understood, for the first time, what it was truly like to need a man's body.

She moved against him. "I want you, Shane."

His hands stilled instantly. He lay with the top half of his body covering hers. His breathing was rough in her ear. "No." He pushed away, ignoring her attempts to pull him back to her. He turned his head. "Cover yourself."

She did, with hands that were shaking so badly she hardly had the coordination to manage. When she had slipped back into her gown, she put a tentative hand on his arm. He shook it off. "I'm not going to let you take the easy way out, mockingbird."

She bit her lip, fully understanding what he meant. He was right and she was desperately ashamed.

He went on. "We'd make love, and you, having been raised the way you were, would feel compelled to marry me. Your decision would be made for you."

"I wanted you."

"Either I didn't teach you enough, or I taught you too much seven years ago." His voice was cold, and he stood as he said the words. "Desire's important, but it's not enough."

"Desire's not enough. Love's not enough. What is enough?"

"Commitment. It's the one thing we don't have going for us."

"Commitment means two people working together to find solutions to their problems. You have never given an inch, Shane. You want me to give up all my dreams for you." Wendy threw back the covers and sat on the edge of the bed to face him.

"Name me one compromise we can make. I'll be glad to meet you halfway. Tell me how I can be a farmer and live in the city with you. Find a way and I'll do it."

"We could get married and I could commute home on weekends."

"Half a wife is not better than none."

"You could buy a farm closer to the city."

"Have you priced land? The closer you get, the more it skyrockets. I couldn't begin to replace the land I have now."

"I think I could go on making suggestions into the night, and you'd shoot down every one of them," she said wearily. "You really don't want me, do you?"

There was a long silence and finally, "No, mockingbird. I'm not sure I do."

Her eyes were stricken with grief, and she raised them to his in mute appeal.

"I don't know if I could stand to watch our love wither every day," he said quietly. "We would compromise, and compromise and compromise, and neither of us would be happy. Then one morning we'd wake up and realize that we'd compromised our love away. Just like that. And by then, it would be too late to do anything about it."

She had pushed him into saying the words she least wanted to hear. It was too much; she couldn't take any more. "I think you'd better go."

He nodded. "Will you be all right?"

"I'll be all right. Thank you for coming. Please tell my parents I'll call them tomorrow." She knew how formal she sounded, but somehow it seemed appropriate. They were nothing more than strangers, after all. Strangers who would probably avoid each other forever after.

"I didn't come here to hurt you."

"In the future, please don't come at all." She stood and walked unsteadily to the door, opening it to usher him out. "Goodbye, Shane."

"Take care of yourself, Wendy."

"If I don't, Shane, it won't be your concern, will it?" She tried to shut the door, but he made it impossible.

"If you think about what I've said, you'll see how right I am."

"I'm sure you're right, Shane." She looked him straight in the eye as she delivered her parting words. "If being married to you was even half as miserable as being in love with you has been, we'd be divorced in a week. I'm glad you had the sense to realize it. Best of luck with Nancy." This time when she tried to close the door, he let her.

She leaned against it, listening to the sound of Shane's footsteps descending the stairs. It took her long minutes to get up the strength to find her way back to bed.

Chapter Ten

There was no reason to pull the covers over her head. It was Saturday, an absolutely perfect morning in June, and Atlanta flourished in green splendor outside Wendy's apartment window.

So, if that was true, why was she lying in bed with the sheet pulled up to her eyebrows, dreading the day to come?

She began to list the reasons.

Number one. She had stayed up much too late the night before at a going-away party for Darcy. Darcy and Donnie-boy had decided to tie the knot again, and Darcy was moving to Kentucky. As a wedding present to her soon-to-be husband, Darcy had thrown away all the libelous chapters in her autobiography that dealt with the world of horse racing.

Number two. Today was the beginning of a two-week vacation that Wendy didn't want. There was no place she wanted to be, no one she wanted to be with. Correction.

There was no one she wanted to be with who also wanted to be with her.

Number three. The city, a source of seemingly endless joy, had gotten stale. It wasn't that she didn't like it anymore. She would always love Atlanta. It was just that every day she realized more and more that buildings and interesting stores and good restaurants did not spell home.

She wanted to go back to Hall County. She wanted to be with people who remembered what she had looked like when she lost her first tooth and people who still told stories about the time she tied up one of her twin brothers in the woods and forgot to rescue him at the end of the game.

How long had she felt this way? It was hard to tell. It was all mixed up in her struggle for independence and the pressure she had gotten from the man she loved. Nothing was clear to her anymore. Not her feelings, her dreams, nor the plans for her life. She was muddling through each day, doing the best she could. But it wasn't enough.

"Come on, Wendy," she cajoled the rebellious woman under the sheet. "Get up, get going. Today is the first day of the rest of your life." What a gloomy thought that was.

She swung her legs over the side of the bed and pulled on shorts and a T-shirt that were lying in a heap on the floor. Her morning toilet consisted of running her fingers through her tousled curls. Her hair was longer than it had been in years. After her one and only experience in an Atlanta salon, she was afraid to have it cut again. This time she feared she might end up with a Mohawk.

To tempt an appetite that had become increasingly difficult to tempt, she made an omelet with two different imported cheeses. She ground her own Jamaican coffee beans, put them in an elaborate pot and poured boiling water over them. It seemed the height of sophistication, but a new friend had informed her that the "best" way to make coffee was to concoct a special syrup from coffee and cold water. It had something to do with acids, and caffeine and superior flavor. Actually, Wendy couldn't care less. Using any method to make coffee for one person was too much trouble.

While the coffee dripped she went for the paper and the mail. Mail from home was rare, but today she was lucky. There was a letter from her mother. Wendy made herself finish half the omelet before she opened the letter. It was a reward for good behavior. The letter was full of news about the family. Bonnie was walking by herself now; Stacey's new baby was precious and looked exactly like his brother, Devin; Sarah was home for the summer, this time in charge of the car counting operation for the whole county. Sarah might become one of Hall County's most influential citizens. Soon she would know everyone's secrets.

As always, there was no mention of Shane. That meant that three more months had gone by without a word about the man Wendy loved. Wendy wondered if, when Shane married Nancy, Mrs. MacDonald would let her daughter know. As she tried to put the letter back in the envelope, she guessed that her mother, without personal comment, would send her a newspaper clipping about the wedding. It would be a newspaper clipping just like the one folded at the bottom of the envelope in her hand. Wendy stared at the small, folded piece of newsprint. She hadn't noticed it at first. It had been stuck in a corner.

She put the envelope next to her place mat and forced herself to finish the now-cold omelet. She wasn't saving this particular piece of paper as a reward. She simply couldn't make herself read the bad news. She washed her dishes and then returned to the table.

If it was an announcement of Shane's wedding, she wouldn't scream or cry. She would simply go out on her porch and take a flying leap. Of course the porch was screened-in and only one story off the ground, but Wendy wasn't going to let small details interfere.

"Melange Gets New Owner." The *Times* article was short and to the point. Helen Merritt was moving to Clarkesville and she had sold her gift shop to an undisclosed buyer. There was no indication what the new owner would do with it. The store was temporarily closed.

Wendy folded the article and put it back in the envelope with her mother's letter. She was saying a soft prayer of thanks when she realized what she was doing. She had no right. No right in the world. Shane deserved happiness. One of them deserved it, at least. There was no point in both of them being miserable and lonely.

She was staring at the coffee cup when there was a knock at her front door. No one, except Darcy, had just dropped by since Wendy had moved to Atlanta. And Darcy had caught a plane to Kentucky before dawn. Still, Wendy wasn't even curious. She was too depressed to be curious.

She opened the door. The young woman standing there looked vaguely familiar. "Wendy? I hope I'm not disturbing you." The young woman took in Wendy's rumpled shorts and equally rumpled hair. Wendy knew she looked disturbed.

"No. Come on in."

"I'm glad I found you. I don't know my way around Atlanta very well."

It was Nancy Gwynn. All wholesome, neatly dressed five-foot-seven inches of her. Wendy wondered how she could ever have forgotten that face. "Come have some coffee, Nancy."

Nancy sat at the little table that Wendy had bought in April to finish furnishing her apartment. Now everything she owned was new, and attractive and...sterile. At the thought, Wendy set Nancy's cup down too hard and sloshed coffee on her own wrist. She barely felt it.

"What brings you here?" she asked as she sat across from Nancy and folded her hands under her chin. It was a casual posture, just right for the occasion. It also held her chin up, and her chin needed to be held up.

"I'm going to get right to the point."

Wendy nodded. It would be absurd to pretend that she had any reason in the world to have a friendly chat with this woman. "Good."

"I want to know what your intentions are regarding Shane."

The question was certainly to the point. Wendy couldn't answer. She hadn't thought she had any right to have intentions.

Nancy waited until it was obvious that Wendy was at a loss for words. She sat back in her chair and folded her arms. "I'm going to level with you. Shane and I have been seeing each other for quite a while. I think we'll marry eventually if no one interferes. But Shane loves someone else, and I think that someone is you."

Wendy could feel her cheeks getting hot. Before she could answer, she had to understand something. "How can you discuss this so calmly? Do you love Shane?"

Nancy looked suddenly tired. "Yes, I love him. But I'm not 'in love' with him. Does that make sense to you?"

Wendy shook her head.

Nancy continued. "I was in love once. With my husband. It was magic. I don't feel that way about Shane. We share a common life-style and common values. I know he'll make a good husband, a good father for Robby, and

I know I'll make him a good wife. But it's different than it was the first time."

Wendy slapped her hand on the table, surprising them both. She couldn't believe that this woman could be so blasé about the man Wendy loved. "How can you say that! Shane is the sexiest, most attractive man I've ever met and I've met a lot of men. There's something wrong with you if you're not head over heels in love with him!"

"If you feel that way, why are you sitting here in Atlanta?" Nancy slapped the table, too. "Come back to Hall County and stake your claim, lady, or don't ever come back again. I'm not going to let you string Shane along anymore. I swear if you're not back in the picture again in a week, I'll convince him to marry me." The two women glared at each other.

Finally Nancy stood. "I was married to a man I'd die for. That'll probably only happen once in my life. Shane deserves to have that experience too. But if you're not willing to give it to him, I'll give him what I can." She gave an exaggerated, lewd wink that was completely incongruous on her all-American face. "And Wendy, once we're married, I'll be sure I'm enough for Shane. You can count on that."

The door didn't slam, nor did it close gently. Wendy was left alone with Nancy's ultimatum echoing in the air around her.

"So what do you think? Should I give up my dreams and go back home with my tail between my legs?"

The squirrel continued to sit on the branch above Wendy's head. She decided that he was probably too old or too sick to find anything better to do than listen to a half-crazed woman tell him the story of her life.

After Nancy left, Wendy had changed into clean clothes and locked her apartment behind her. She couldn't bear to sit around her quiet apartment and think. She had driven around the city for an hour, and now she was standing in one of Atlanta's fine little parks—she didn't even know which one—and she was talking to a squirrel she had never met before. At least at home in Hall County if she was desperate enough to talk to a four-legged creature, she would have had her pick of dogs and cats she had known forever.

The squirrel didn't understand her. It was the story of her life. No one had ever understood her. She was an anomaly. In a family of hardworking, sensible people she had danced to different music. She hadn't been criticized for it; she had been accepted and loved as much for her differences as for any other reason. She couldn't quarrel with the way she had been brought up. But with different parenting, she would have grown up to be a rebel, like Shane. Instead she had done the things a good daughter is supposed to do, and she had chafed at the bit until she was given her freedom.

Now she had all the freedom any one person would ever need. And if she chose to make freedom the most important thing in her life, she could have it until the day she died. Complete and total freedom.

It had its charms. For the first time in Wendy's life she wasn't being asked to live up to anyone else's expectations. She had certain standards to maintain on her job, but the rest of her life was her own.

Except that it wasn't. Not really. She had expectations of herself that she couldn't ignore. Those expectations demanded that she behave a certain way, and she was as bound by them as she would have been if she was still living with her parents. She was free to pursue a free and easy life-style, but she wouldn't. She didn't want to. For better or worse, she was Wendy MacDonald, daughter of Raymond and Eldora MacDonald. And she was satisfied to be that person.

"So why is freedom so important?"

The squirrel tired of Wendy's ceaseless chatter and ran up to a higher limb. Wendy sat down on the grass beneath the tree and leaned against its trunk. She might not be free to behave any way she wanted, but at least she was free to follow her dreams. But what were her dreams?

Nothing came to mind. She had never realized just how nebulous her life plans were. She did not have a burning desire to pursue a profession. Her sister Sandy had wanted to become a lawyer; Sarah wanted to be a college professor. Neither of them wanted to settle for anything less. There were any number of things Wendy knew she would be happy doing.

She liked decorating the world. It wasn't a passion, it was an interest, one that she could carry out anywhere in a number of different ways. She didn't have to be a manager or an executive in a high-level position with one of the bigger gift store companies. She liked working with customers; she liked handling the merchandise herself and giving advice.

So why was she in Atlanta? She had been happy working at Melange, happier than she had ever been in her job with Atlanta Card and Gift Stores. One of her dreams had been the glamour of the city. But she didn't have to live here to enjoy that. No evening she had ever spent here had been more fun, more exciting than her first and last date with Shane. Being in the city with someone you loved increased its attractions one hundred fold.

"All this time, I've been rebelling." She couldn't believe it. She didn't want to believe it. Why?

Wendy stood and wandered through the little park. There had to be more to this year's experience than that. She sat on a stone bench beneath two big trees and closed her eyes. There were street noises, cars and buses whizzing by, someone passing with a large radio on his shoulder, birds singing.

There was a mockingbird in the tree above her. His song was vibrant and alive. And not his own.

How did the mockingbird find his own call? How did Wendy MacDonald find hers?

She knew what her call was not. It was not working from sunup to sundown and raising twelve children as her mother had willingly done. It was not dedicating herself exclusively to home and hearth and six children as Stacey was doing. It was not pursuing a riveting career as it was for Sandy. And it was not... it was not living in Atlanta, lonely and miserable and aching for the man she loved.

She could choose what fit for her. Every song in history was assembled from the notes of other songs. It was the way they were assembled that made them unique.

Wendy stood and began to pace the perimeter of the park, around and around, her feet moving faster as the truth began to dawn on her. She had been so busy trying not to be like the people she saw around her, she had completely dismissed the parts of their lives that would fit for her. It had started when she had felt that Shane had abandoned her. She had decided that she would never be vulnerable, and not being vulnerable meant being sophisticated, being different from the people she cared about.

Wendy became so excited at the thoughts tumbling around in her head that she began to jog. With her eyes riveted on the ground in front of her she missed the smiles of passing strangers who were staring at the lovely young woman, curls bouncing in disarray as she ran faster and faster down the sidewalk.

Wendy had thought that if she got away from home she would be free. Well, now she was. No one was making her decisions for her. Shane had set her free to find herself. He had loved her enough to give her the room she needed. It was the best kind of love because he got nothing in return for it. He had respected her dreams and respected his own dreams, too.

She had almost lost him because of his own generosity. When she had wavered, he had pushed her away. He had known that no matter how much he wanted her, only having part of her would not be enough.

She ran and ran until finally, totally exhausted, she threw herself at the foot of the tree where she had reeled off a monologue to the squirrel.

For the first time in her life, she understood the simplest truth in the world. She could be the person she wanted to be, but in order to be that person, she had to stop rebelling and she had to stop imitating. It was time for the real Wendy MacDonald to stand up and be counted. The mockingbird was on the spot.

And if she was still a little confused about who the real Wendy MacDonald was, she was absolutely sure of one thing. The real Wendy MacDonald was going to go home to find the answers. Because that's where they had been all along.

"Look at all those stars. Where did those stars come from?"

"They've been here every night of your life, Wendy. You were the child who was always out here watching them." Eldora MacDonald rocked quietly back and forth, watching the daughter who was seated on the top porch step stretch her arms to the sky. Eldora was still trying to adjust to the fact that Wendy had come home that day and announced that she was staying on the farm for her whole vacation.

Wendy gave a delighted laugh. "I was always wishing on those stars. Wishing I was somebody else, somewhere else. I'm not sure I ever saw them for what they are. Stars. Beautiful, beautiful stars."

"You've been high as a kite all day."

"I've been on the edge of a discovery." Wendy's mouth widened into a broad grin. "I'm setting myself free."

Mrs. MacDonald shook her head. "When you come back to earth, explain it to me."

"Wendy's trying to tell you that she's finally realized where she belongs." Sarah came out on the porch to join them, and Wendy patted the step beside her.

"You're right, as usual," Wendy said, giving her sister an impromptu hug. "Why didn't you just tell me and save me all this agony?"

"Because no one has every been able to tell you anything. You'd run the other way in protest."

"I never realized that about myself until today."

"I don't understand a word of this," Mrs. MacDonald said. "But if this new discovery has put the sparkle back in your eyes, honey, I'm all for it."

"The sparkle's only half there, Ma. I get the rest back when I ask Shane to marry me."

Mrs. MacDonald stopped rocking. "What?"

"As soon as Shane agrees to marry me, I'll have all my sparkle back." Wendy smiled at her mother. "Maybe that will even happen tomorrow."

"You're pretty sure of yourself, aren't you?" Sarah asked.

"Actually I'm scared to death."

"Good. He's not going to be easy to convince."

"What are you two girls talking about?" Mrs. Mac-Donald was completely confused.

"It's simple, Ma." Sarah was patient. "Wendy has been in love with Shane since she was sixteen. They had a mis-understanding and Shane disappeared. Then he came back and they realized that they were still in love. But Wendy had made other plans for her life by then, and she resented Shane's interference in them. So she's spent most of the past year in Atlanta finding out that her plans weren't really worth doodley-squat. Now she's back to tell Shane that he's the only thing that really matters to her."

"Oh." Mrs. MacDonald was quiet for a moment. Then, "Sarah, how did I raise such a know-it-all?"

Sarah shrugged. "Beats me. But aren't you glad somebody keeps track of everything for you?"

"I've never regretted it for a moment." Mrs. Mac-Donald addressed Wendy. "Is Sarah right?"

"Almost. Shane is not the only thing that really matters to me. I have needs and interests of my own. But I've just realized for the first time how flexible they are. My love for Shane isn't flexible, however. I'm going to tell him that tomorrow."

"And you're going to be a farmer's wife?"

"If the farmer will have me."

"And if he won't?" Sarah asked.

"Then I'm going to make his life miserable until he changes his mind."

There was only one more thing that Wendy felt compelled to do before she went to bed that night. When everyone else had gone to sleep, she turned off all the lights downstairs and went into the kitchen. By the light of one small lamp she found Nancy's telephone and dialed it.

"Hello."

Wendy was delighted to find that Nancy had answered on the first ring. She had imagined the telephone ringing and ringing in the empty house. She had imagined Nancy in Shane's arms and in Shane's bed.

"Hello, Nancy. This is Wendy MacDonald."

There was a short pause. "I have a feeling you're not calling from Atlanta," Nancy said finally.

"That's right. I thought it only fair to tell you that I'm back in town, and I'm going after Shane."

Nancy's voice was surprisingly cordial. In fact, Wendy almost thought she was muffling a giggle. "Well, is that so? I'll wish you the best of luck then. I'm going to be out of town for the next week, so we won't be running into each other. You have a clear shot if you want it."

Clear shot indeed. "You don't have to do me any favors," Wendy said sweetly.

"Coming to Atlanta to warn you about my intentions was my favor, honey. The rest is up to you. Have a good week."

The line went dead.

Wendy stared at the receiver, and suddenly she realized that she wasn't done making phone calls. Nancy knew she was back, but Shane did not. She had lived with his presence all day. Now she had to hear his voice.

She took a deep breath as she looked up his number. She was not surprised to find that it was one of those posted on a small bulletin board next to the telephone along with all the numbers of her closest relatives.

Her finger trembled as she dialed.

"Hello." Shane's voice was husky with sleep. Wendy realized she had woken him up.

"Hello, Shane. This is Wendy."

"Wendy." He sounded as if he were drifting back to dreamland.

"Yes, Wendy MacDonald." *You know, the love of your life*. "How are you?"

"Damned tired."

There was silence on the line. Wendy couldn't think of anything to say. Finally she asked, like an idiot, "Have you had a hard day?"

This time he grunted in response as if he were too exhausted to open his mouth.

Where were the tender words they were going to exchange? Where were the sweet nothings she wanted to have whispered in her ear? Where was polite conversation? Wendy's disappointment turned into anger. "Well, I won't keep you any longer, Shane. It's been lovely talking to you. We'll have to do it again in about a hundred years."

She slammed the receiver into place with a resounding bang. She hoped she had finally gotten Shane's attention. If she hadn't, she would the next day when she went to see him to give him a piece of her mind.

"Shane Reynolds," she said to nothing in particular, "if you think you're going to play hard to get with me again, you have another think coming. Get a good night's sleep, my love, because tomorrow you're going to find out just exactly what you're up against. Not only have I found my own call, I'm going to sing it in stereo!"

Chapter Eleven

Wendy was staring glumly at her coffee cup when her mother came downstairs to start Raymond MacDonald's breakfast.

"I've spent more time staring at coffee lately," Wendy muttered. "If I knew how to read coffee grounds, I'd be in business for myself."

"What happened to your high spirits? One egg or two?"

Wendy shook her head. "Nothing for me, thank you. I talked to Shane last night. I don't think he remembered who I was." She had awakened before dawn. Her determination to make Shane listen to her had evaporated sometime during the night. Now she only felt resigned to the inevitable. She would make the attempt to see him, but her expectations had plummeted.

"I can tell you why he probably didn't sound interested. But maybe you're feeling too sorry for yourself to listen."

Wendy's head snapped up, and she stared at her mother.

"I thought that might get your attention," Mrs. MacDonald said, flashing her daughter a big smile. "Now, since you didn't get a good night's sleep, you'll have to have a good breakfast to compensate. Two eggs or three?"

Wendy knew when she'd been bested. "Two, please." Accepting defeat was better than having her mother steadily increase her offer of eggs to an even dozen.

"I talked to your father about Shane last night as we were falling asleep." Mrs. MacDonald turned down the heat under the grits and flipped the sausage patties before she turned to face Wendy. "Shane is in big trouble."

"What's wrong?" Wendy had to consciously stop herself from throwing her hands to her face in a melodramatic gesture of horror. She wove her fingers together and put her hands on the table in front of her.

"He bit off more than he could chew. A lot more. Seems he's been working like the devil this year. Almost as if he were trying to forget something, or somebody."

Wendy lowered her eyes.

"Anyway," Mrs. MacDonald went on, "the Reynolds' farm was a real disaster by the time Shane came back to claim it. His father really let it go and concentrated on his investments and his real estate instead. When Shane came back and saw the mess it was in, he decided to fix it all at once. Your father told him to take it easy, start with the broiler houses, then do the pastures, then his crops, then on to the orchards. But Shane wanted to do it all. According to your daddy, the last straw was this organic plot he's been experimenting with."

"Go on."

"Well, it's all caught up with him now. One of his men quit, said Shane was working him too hard. He hired another man, but he won't be much good until he knows his way around a little. Shane's chickens all go to market this week, and though he's hired extra help to catch and crate them, that's going to take all his energy. In the meantime two of his cows are sick and need constant surveillance, his peach trees have developed leaf spot because they were neglected so long and they've got to be sprayed immediately...." Mrs MacDonald stopped. "I could go on and on. Probably the worst for Shane, though, is that bollworms are on the move. His organic patch is going to be the first thing they attack."

"And he can't spray because then it wouldn't be organic." Wendy could just imagine how Shane must feel.

"Your father told him to spray his pastures. That's where the worms hatch out. If pastures are kept close and taken care of, you don't have as much trouble with any kind of cutworm. But Shane's pastures were shoulder high when he came back. The damage had been done. And he wasn't willing to spray anything close to where he was going to have his organic vegetables. Now it looks as if he's going to have to spray the vegetables unless he wants to lose the whole crop."

"He must feel awful right now." Wendy was regretting her angry words on the telephone.

"Your father says he's been working right around the clock. He's probably too exhausted to feel much of anything." Mrs. MacDonald drained the sausage and cracked eggs in the frying pan. As if on cue, Mr. MacDonald came into the kitchen.

"Morning." He poured himself a cup of coffee. Wendy knew that he had already been up for an hour taking care of the most immediate chores. Breakfast was just a break.

"Morning, Daddy." Wendy set the table for the three of them as she thought about her mother's words. "Ma was telling me about Shane," she said when breakfast was on the table.

"Your ma seems to think you're sweet on him. Is that right?" Mr. MacDonald bit into a biscuit.

"That's right. I'm going to ask him to marry me."

Mr. MacDonald stopped chewing. "Is that so?"

"Today. In between the cows and chickens and the bollworms."

"You'd better think long and hard about it. Look around. Being a farmer's wife isn't real glamorous. And make no mistake about it, that boy is a farmer through and through."

"And you are looking at a Grade A farmer's daughter who knows exactly what she's doing." Wendy finished her breakfast in two big gulps. "Are you using the little boys today?"

Mr. MacDonald snorted. The "little boys"—Timothy, eighteen, and Danny, sixteen—were both six inches taller than Wendy. "No. With James and Randy home for the summer, I can spare them. Why?"

"How about Jennifer?"

"I can spare Jennifer," Mrs. MacDonald said.

"Good. Will you tell them to come to Shane's house about nine-thirty, dressed to work? And tell Jennifer to bring her organic gardening books with her." Wendy was halfway out of the kitchen before she yelled back, "Tell them I'll pay them minimum wage."

Shane's house was a mess. And Shane was nowhere to be seen. Wendy shook her head at the disorder as she walked through the downstairs. She suspected that Shane had left the house unlocked in the hopes that some good-hearted burglar would drive a moving van up to the front door and load everything, mess and all, to haul it away for him.

The kitchen was by far the worst of the disasters. There was a week's worth of dirty dishes stacked in the sink, frozen dinner packages littering the counters and an open box of presweetened breakfast cereal on the table. The refrigerator was almost empty.

There was one optimistic note that shone through the depressing jumble. Obviously Nancy Gwynn had not been there for a long, long time.

Forty-five minutes later Wendy found Shane in the barn. She stood in the doorway and watched as he concentrated on the cow in front of him. She had never seen him look so tired, so worn, so utterly gorgeous. He was wearing an old flannel shirt that he hadn't bothered to button and a pair of jeans that were so stiff with dust that they would have stood by themselves. She guessed he hadn't shaved for a week and the resulting beard looked as if it belonged on a skid row bum. None of that mattered to Wendy. She saw only the same beautiful body, the same arresting eyes.

The one thing that did matter was the look of weary defeat on his face as he stared at the cow.

"Shane?"

He turned slightly and she saw him will his eyes to focus on her. He didn't say a word, just silently took in her faded jeans and T-shirt, the bandanna she had used to cover her curls, the cardboard box she held in front of her like a shield.

"You can't do a decent day's work on a bowl of Chocolate Crunchy Stars or whatever that nonsense on the table was," she chastised him softly. "I brought you breakfast." She advanced slowly as if she were approaching a dog suspected of having rabies. When he didn't do anything except stare, she gained a little confidence.

"You didn't have much in your refrigerator," she said as she got closer. "But I made you scrambled eggs with

cheese and toast. There's a thermos of coffee in here, too."
She looked at his hands and wrinkled her nose. "And soap
and clean towels."

She set the box on the ground in front of him. "Can you
think of anything else you need right this minute?"

Shane drew his brows together as if he were trying hard
to understand why she was there and what she was talking
about.

"Okay," Wendy said cheerfully. "I'll see you later
then." Before he found his voice she was gone.

The house desperately needed to be cleaned, but Wendy
knew it would have to wait for another day. She concentrated her efforts on the kitchen, hauling out garbage,
washing dishes, scrubbing the counters and floor until they
shone. By 8:00 A.M. she had made an extensive grocery list
and was on her way to Gainesville to shop. By nine she was
back at the house putting carrots in a huge kettle of beef
stew.

Jennifer and the boys arrived right on time. Jennifer was
already one step ahead of her sister. "I know what to do
for bollworms," she said before Wendy could explain her
request. "But it's going to be a whole lot of work."

"How did you know what I wanted?"

"Daddy guessed. He thinks we're crazy, but he says he'll
come help tonight if we're still working."

Jennifer outlined her plan, and Wendy groaned. "Isn't
there some other way? Can't we just spray with something we make up ourselves from garlic or marigold blossoms or something?"

"You've been reading!"

Wendy had to admit it. She had been reading about organic gardening for the past six months. It had become an
obsession she hadn't understood very well. Certainly it
didn't benefit her bromeliads.

"But Wendy," Jennifer continued, "you've got to think big. This is five acres we're talking about. Not someone's backyard. We can't put a bunch of stuff in Shane's blender and expect to kill an army of bollworms."

By noon they had been to the feed store, the local sorghum distributor and the lumber mill. They had filled one of the MacDonald pickups with a mixture of hardwood sawdust, wheat bran and molasses. Timothy and Daniel made disgusting remarks as they trained hoses on the mixture to saturate it.

"Time for lunch, boys," Wendy called sweetly from the house. "If you still have any appetite that is."

This time she found Shane in one of the broiler houses. If possible, he looked even more exhausted. "I've brought lunch," she said. "Enough for everybody."

Shane and the five men helping him catch chickens filed out. It was not a pretty sight. As they washed under a hose, Wendy ladled stew into plastic bowls and heaped biscuits on a plate. A jug of sweetened tea completed the menu. She served from the trunk of her car. Shane was the last in line.

"Wendy, what are you doing here?" The words were issued through clenched teeth.

It was an improvement. He had not lost his voice.

"I thought that was obvious," she said.

"You know what I mean!"

Wendy couldn't resist. She stepped within touching distance and patted the rough stubble on Shane's cheek. "We'll talk later. Right now I've got the world's largest batch of cereal up at the house waiting for me to take care of it." Before he could respond, she stood on tiptoe and kissed his sweaty nose. "I'll see you at supper."

Wendy had never ached so in her life. Each shovelful of dirt hurt more than the last one had. "We're almost done," she encouraged her siblings.

Jennifer, whose enthusiasm was unflagging, leaned on her shovel and applauded. "It's almost dusk. My book said that the best time to spread the bran bait is at dusk because that way it stays damp all night."

Only Jennifer could find anything to be enthused about. Wendy and Danny and Timothy were only exhausted. They had dug a two-feet-deep trench all along the side of Shane's vegetable plot that faced his pastureland. They had plowed first with an old-fashioned hand plow they found in the barn, but the last few inches had been done solely by shovel and sweat.

"That's it." Timothy put down his shovel. "I'm not doing another inch. It's time to spread the bran."

"I hope there's enough." Wendy bit her lip.

"If there's not, we can mix more and spread it again tomorrow evening," Jennifer said cheerfully.

Everyone else groaned.

As they spread the bran on the side of the trench by the pasture, Wendy pictured the army of bollworms crawling through the bran. They would be attracted by the molasses and roll their nasty little bodies around in the mixture. By morning it would harden and render them helpless to the ravages of the wind and sun and birds. Those worms who made it past the bait would fall into the trench where they could be relentlessly extinguished the next morning.

"Goodbye bollworms!" Wendy shouted as the last shovelful of bran hit the ground. "Thanks kids. Now you all go home and get some supper. Ask Ma if she'll save some for Shane and me. I'm going to make him quit working long enough to eat."

Wendy waved as they drove away. Then she turned to go up to the house.

She had hoped to beat Shane back. Although she hadn't thought to bring a change of clothes, she wanted to at least wash the dirt and bran from her face and hands. She was sunburned, wet with perspiration and completely unlovable. It was no way to propose to the man she wanted to spend her life with.

On the front porch she listened for sounds inside. The house was silent. She let herself in and tiptoed toward the downstairs bathroom. In the hallway she collided with Shane who was coming from the direction of the kitchen.

His hair was wet as if he had just showered, and he was freshly shaved. His clothes were clean. "What are you still doing here?" he asked, holding her at arm's length.

"I've been getting rid of your bollworms."

The look on his face was somewhere on the continuum between fury and rage. "You've been doing what?" Holding one hand he dragged her stumbling body toward the bathroom. "You little fool! What kind of dumb stunt is this?" He slammed the door behind them and stood against it. "Get in that shower!"

Wendy couldn't believe it. She knew she wasn't at her best but she didn't believe that hot water and soap were that much of an emergency. Not enough to inspire this kind of violence. She tried to placate him. "Sure. But don't you think you'd better leave first?"

He folded his arms over his chest and shook his head. "Turn that water on right now or I'll throw you in myself."

"I'm not going to undress with you in here." She could be stubborn, too.

"You're not going to undress at all. Get in with your clothes on. Then hand them to me when they're clean."

Had Shane gone kinky? Wendy just stared until Shane began to advance. "All right. All right." She turned on the water full blast and began to take off her tennis shoes.

"Leave your shoes on. Get in that shower right now."

Wendy did as she was told, convinced that lack of sleep had finally pushed Shane over the edge. Under the driving beat of the water she tried to relax. She had seen enough Alfred Hitchcock movies to know what could happen to young women in showers, but she trusted Shane even when he seemed to have lost his mind. To soothe his shattered nerves, she tried to sing a chorus of "I'm Gonna Wash That Man" as she washed her hair with Shane's shampoo.

"Your clothes, Wendy. Take off your clothes."

She was tempted to refuse, but she had a feeling that Shane wasn't going to let her. She stripped down to nothing but her underclothes and passed her shirt and jeans to him over the top of the shower curtain.

"You're not done!"

"Nothing else goes!"

"I'll do it myself then!"

"No, wait." She finished undressing and threw her bra and panties over the shower curtain like a stripper whose act has just come to a close. "There. Are you satisfied?"

There was no answer. Shane was gone.

Wendy turned off the water and gingerly stepped out of the bathtub. She locked the door and found a towel. When she was dry, she wrapped it around her newly clean body like a sarong. Then she sat on the edge of the tub, wondering what she should do next. She was locked in Shane's bathroom without her clothing. This could be very difficult to explain to her mother.

"Wendy, open the door. I've got something for you to wear."

Should she trust the man who had asked her to shower fully clothed and then had taken every single stitch away piece by piece? "First tell me why this was necessary."

"Don't be an idiot!"

"Look who's talking!"

"Wendy, open that door. I'm too tired to play games." Shane waited. She was silent. Wendy could hear his exasperated sigh through the door. "I made you take a shower because you were covered with poison. That stuff gets in every pore, it permeates your clothes. You're a city girl. You don't understand these things."

She still didn't understand. How could bran and molasses and sawdust poison anything? "Shane, are you all right?" she asked softly. She remembered that exhaustion could actually cause hallucinations. She wondered if he was in the grip of one.

"Open the damned door."

This time she complied. She turned the knob and stuck her hand through the resulting crack. Something soft brushed her fingertips. When she pulled her hand back through she was holding an oversize work shirt. Buttoned on her petite body, it trailed down to stop at midthigh. Acutely aware that underneath it she was naked, Wendy turned the doorknob again and stepped out of the bathroom.

"What poison?" she asked.

Shane's eyes roamed her body as he answered. "The poison you used to spray the bollworms. The stuff the feed store delivered today."

Relief flooded her face and her voice. She stepped closer. "Nobody delivered any poison that I know of. I didn't spray anything. Jennifer, Daniel, Timothy and I dug a trench and baited it with molasses and bran and sawdust all mixed together. It's supposed to..."

He was advancing slowly. "I know what it's supposed to do." He watched her blink as he stopped in front of her. "I'm sorry I jumped to conclusions."

"I'm just glad you haven't lost your mind."

For a moment a smile hovered at the corners of his mouth. Then his face turned grim again. "Now what I want to know is what you're doing here. You're a city girl. Is this some kind of fun and games vacation for you?"

"Believe me, this has been no vacation." Wendy turned her palms up for him to examine. They were a mass of blisters from her encounter with the shovel. "I'm not a city girl anymore. I'm back to stay. With you."

He lifted an eyebrow. "Why? Did you lose your job? Your boyfriend?"

Wendy understood Shane's distrust. Along with almost everyone else in his life, she had helped to foster it.

"My job's fine. In fact I got a raise recently. I guess you'll have to be the one to tell me if I've lost my boyfriend." She lifted her hand and it took the same path that it had taken that afternoon. She smoothed her fingertips over his cheek. "I'm back because I love you, and this is the only place in the world that I want to be."

Shane shut his eyes, and Wendy smoothed her fingertips over his eyelids. "Are you sure?" he asked softly. "Because I'm not going to be able to let you go again."

"Absolutely sure. I'm here for good. As your wife if you'll have me."

"I'll have you." Shane wrapped his arms around her and pulled her close. His voice was rough. "Right now the problem is going to be how to *keep* from having you until we can make it legal."

Wendy's entire body reacted to his words. With a glad cry, she threw her arms around Shane's neck and pulled his mouth down to hers. She covered his lips and his chin with tiny kisses until he held her still to fasten his mouth over hers. His tongue parried hers, and his body shuddered with feeling. He clasped her tightly, lifting her against him, and the kiss went on and on.

"God, sweetheart, there's not much left to the imagination in that shirt." He set her down and backed away.

She smiled and closed the space between them again. "It's not my fault, you know. You're the one who made me strip."

"Do you know how I felt when I thought you'd been out there wallowing in pesticide?" He hugged her hard and then pulled away again.

"I was out saving our crops on our land for our children."

"That has a ring to it, doesn't it." Shane laughed as she snuggled against him. Finally he pushed her away to take her hand and lead her into the living room.

"This place needs to be fumigated," Wendy said with her nose in the air.

"You can do anything you want to it. I give you free rein." Shane sat in a big armchair and pulled Wendy on his lap. Her bare legs dangled over his, and she carefully adjusted the shirt around them. "Now tell me what brought you back."

"I found my song."

Shane couldn't seem to stop touching her. His hands explored her hair, which was drying in fluffy curls around her face. His mouth explored her cheeks, her ears, the back of her neck. As if he'd made a vow to himself, however, he ignored the tempting flesh beneath her shirt. "Tell me what it is."

"I realized the mockingbird has its own song. It's just made up of parts of everyone else's. So is mine. I want you and children and some kind of career, but one I can pursue here, not away from you. I can be a farmer's wife as long as I can be my own person, too."

"I've never wanted less for you than that." Shane kissed her again and for a long time they were silent.

"Shane, I have to know. What about Nancy?"

"Nancy and I haven't seen each other for a month." He laughed at her indrawn breath. "We both realized that I wasn't going to fall out of love with you."

"But she came to see me in Atlanta. She said that if I stayed out of the picture, she'd get you to marry her."

Shane thought about Wendy's words. When the truth dawned he hooted with laughter. "She was matchmaking. Nancy and I parted as good friends. I think she was trying to get you and me together."

"That sneak!"

"Nancy's great. You'll love her when you get to know her."

Wendy sniffed.

"Don't worry, mockingbird. There'll be a new man in Nancy's life before too long. I wouldn't be surprised if she gets married soon, herself. She's quite a catch."

"It can't be too soon."

"And our wedding?"

"It can't be soon enough." Wendy began to kiss Shane's forehead, his nose, his eyelids. "When the cows are cured and the bollworm threat is over, when the chickens are crated and the broiler houses disinfected, I'll marry you."

"The cows, the chickens." Shane groaned. "I've got five men coming back after supper to finish up."

"I think it's just as well," she teased. "Otherwise you might lose your virtue before I carry you over the threshold."

"We're going to wait this time, my love. We're going to wait until there's no doubt, no fear, no guilt. Until we really belong to each other."

"We already belong to each other. We have since I was sixteen, Shane. Nothing, no words from a preacher, no ring, could make that any less true. If we wait, it's because I don't want to share you with the farm on our first real night together." Wendy pulled his head to her chest and she felt him give way to his weariness. They rested that way for long minutes.

"Shane," she whispered finally. "Are you awake?"

"I'm in heaven."

"Shane, one more thing."

He lifted his head and their eyes held. "From now on," she said, "I'm going to fill your life with more love than you knew it could hold. So you'd better be prepared."

"You already have, mockingbird. And it's been worth waiting for."

"You'll never have to wait again, Shane." Wendy kissed him to seal her promise. "You loved me enough to let me find myself. And now I freely give myself to you. From now on if you need me, I'll be here."

"And I promise that you'll come first, before the land, before the crops." He stopped, as though thinking about his next words. "And I won't stand in your way if you want to manage Melange yourself instead of hiring someone else to do it." Shane pulled Wendy back against his chest and shut his eyes as if to go to sleep.

"Melange?" Wendy pulled his eyes open with her thumbs and forefingers. "What are you talking about, Shane Reynolds?"

"Didn't I tell you?"

Wendy could see that he was enjoying her confusion. "Tell me what!"